CODEX HYPERBOREANUS

YANKO TSVETKOV

CODEX
HYPERBOREANUS

ALPHADESIGNER
Valencia 2019

LILAC FEVER SERIES

CODEX HYPERBOREANUS

Very first edition

Written by Yanko Tsvetkov
in Valencia and Granada

Cover, illustrations, design, and print layout by Yanko Tsvetkov
Copy editing and typesetting by The Illuminati
Art direction by The Powers That Be
Special agent: Martin Brinkmann

Published on May 26, 2019
in Valencia (Spain) by Alphadesigner

ISBN: 978-84-09-09156-0 (ebook)
ISBN: 978-84-09-09155-3 (paperback)
ISBN: 978-84-09-11615-7 (hardcover)

Official website: alphadesigner.com
Facebook: facebook.com/alphadesigner
Instagram: alphadesigner
Twitter: @alphadesigner
Email: alphadesigner@gmail.com

ISNI: 0000 0004 0208 7779
VIAF ID: 296971239

Tho all who have survived being in love

"Fear is the evil twin of love"
Old Hyperborean proverb

Contents

Preface

I vaguely remember the first time I saw a mummy. I was five. My grandma took me to the mausoleum of Georgi Dimitrov, the first communist dictator of Bulgaria. He was laid to rest in a glass-covered sarcophagus—his body hollowed out, pickled by the same experts who mummified Vladimir Lenin in Moscow. It was an awkward sight. Back then, I didn't really know what death was. Communists didn't believe in an afterlife, so every time I asked what happened to people when they stopped breathing, the answer was "Nothing!"

Have you ever tried to imagine a *nothing*? It's not easy, even for a child. "Stop asking questions, or the guards will arrest us!" said my grandma, following an old Bulgarian tradition of using uniformed men as scarecrows. The guards didn't look threatening. They were all young men in pristine white uniforms. Their faces were beautiful but just as lifeless as that of Comrade Dimitrov, who was enjoying a forty years long nap in the middle of the Communist Valhalla.

So many of our aspirations are defined by our desire to freeze time, to preserve everything *as it is supposed to be*. We know it's a losing game, but like compulsive gamblers, we can't quit. For many of us, this game has become our raison d'être. It gives our lives meaning.

Maybe that's why it's so heartbreaking when time decides to remind us who's the boss. Back in the day of our visit to the mausoleum, nobody could imagine that in less than ten years, the corpse inside it would be gone. Even people who despised communism were happy the mummy finally found peace in a common graveyard. Human bodies are fragile by design. They are supposed to be recycled as soon as they have served their purpose.

Buildings, on the other hand, are sturdier. The mausoleum was built in six days. It took longer to demolish it. Despite tons of dynamite and two controlled explosions, it defiantly refused to budge. The third attempt managed to slightly tilt its roof. At that moment, most Bulgarians realized the building was designed to withstand a nuclear strike, so the mummy could outlive us all and possibly repopulate the Earth after the advent of the Zombie Apocalypse. Many considered the demolition ceremony a farce and a humiliation for the democratically elected government that initiated it. But it was more than that. Like a Russian matryoshka doll, it was a farce within a farce within a farce... One could trace it all the way back to the first moment when a primate became aware of his own transience. If there ever was an original sin, it was inspired by nostalgia, not sexual desire.

All things pass, with one exception: some stories are immortal. We're told they stand the test of time because they are unique and deal with eternal subjects. Nothing could be farther from the truth. The greatest stories ever told don't have a real identity. They survive because they constantly adapt. Like viruses, they incorporate the zeitgeist into their own DNA, and morph each time they pass from one mouth to another. Their crowning achievement—if one could ascribe intent to abstractions—is that their mutation happens so fast, we don't even notice it.

Three years ago, driven by nostalgia, I decided to revisit the *Arabian Nights*. I use the word *revisit* intentionally, even though I had never read them before in their entirety. I knew them via adaptations—children's books, animated series, and of course, a few Disney movies. Wouldn't it be wonderful, I thought, if I could go back the memory lane with the eyes of an adult and explore the original versions?

Here's where things became genuinely interesting. There were no original versions of the *Arabian Nights*. It was an embarrassing discovery, one that only seemed logical in retrospect. Few ancient stories have individual authors, and even those who do rarely claim to be original. The modern idea of authorship didn't exist until the advent of capitalism. Just like mass rape, plagiarism was only criminalized in the twentieth century. The *Arabian Nights* are much older. In fact, many of them, including the framing story, abound with characters whose names are unmistakably Persian—Shahrazad is the most obvious example. This unexpected complexity was fascinating.

Looking for authenticity, I began with a translation based on a Syrian manuscript from the fourteenth century. When I finished it, I realized a lot of the emblematic stories were missing. I was told some were added in later versions, compiled in Egypt. Others were suspected to be inventions by Antoine Galland, who is the author of the most popular translation. Among those alleged fakes are the stories of Aladdin, Ali Baba, and Sindbad. Can any contemporary person even imagine the *Arabian Nights* without those characters?

Realizing historical authenticity had nothing to do with my motivation to revisit the stories, I switched to a much longer edition, spanning almost three thousand pages. The familiar characters were all there, but very often, the narratives seemed barely recognizable. Along with magic and wonder, they abounded with unapologetic misogyny, religious intolerance, xenophobia, and glorification of violence. As an explorer of prejudice, I was intrigued, but as a fan of fairy tales, it was impossible to fully immerse myself in them.

Yet instead of a disaster, this misguided adventure turned out to be a source of inspiration. Just like all those storytellers before me, from the ancient Persians to Galland, I took the bits that I liked the most and filtered them through my own creative prism. What reflected back onto the sheet was just another mutation of that ancient virus.

Yanko Tsvetkov
Valencia, May 21, 2019

Terror Birds
and Wanton Hearts

Grandmistress of Fear

 HERE LIVED on the island of Severia a queen that was vicious and dastardly. Her subjects shivered from fear every time they looked at her. Since her terrifying face was engraved on every coin, commercial activity soon ground to a halt, and the once prosperous queendom plunged into the biggest economic depression in its history.

"Your Majesty," said one day the grand vizierienne of the queen, "I realize how important it is to rule with an iron fist and instill respect in the hearts of the masses, but if you value my honest advice, I think that a brief respite—or better yet a loving gesture—might be of great benefit, for it would prevent a possible uprising by an angry mob of disillusioned peasants."

"As my most senior advisor," replied the queen, "you are allowed to speak your mind without fear of my ire, but if I were you, I wouldn't push that privilege too far.

The handrails on the stairs of this palace are quite wobbly. It would be a shame to see you slip and fall over. I still mourn the loss of my treasure secretary, who rolled all the way down from the throne room to the patio like a tumbleweed. Her neck was so brutally fractured, they found her head under her armpit. I heard she was buried in a closed casket."

"Your Majesty," said the grand vizierienne, "I have sworn to serve you in life and death. I fearlessly welcome whatever fate the gods have chosen for me, even if it is to be strangled by my own intestines."

"I expect nothing less from my grand vizierienne," replied the queen, impressed by the dedication of her servant. "State your case in detail, so I can take an informed decision."

"Perhaps the best way to do so is to tell you a story from the queendom of Barbaria," replied the grand vizierienne, for it is full of plot twists that brilliantly illustrate the importance of empathy."

"Speak before I change my mind and throw you to the lions," said the queen and rolled up her sleeves.

And so, the grand vizierienne began her story...

Love in Times of Barbarity

ONCE UPON A TIME, in the lands of Barbaria, there lived an old queen called Dolores. Her advanced age had long eroded the pleasant memories of her youth, as well as all embarrassing mistakes she had made along the way. Every passing second added a tiny wrinkle on her skin, and it wasn't long before her soul lost its joie de vivre. She became intolerant and judgmental, especially to young people, whom she considered careless and irresponsible.

"We don't appreciate life unless we waste the first half of it," she wrote in her diary on her fiftieth birthday.

By the will of the gods, the queen's daughter, Esperanza, fell in love with a miller named Joy, whom she met at a carnival.

"Goodness gracious us," exclaimed Dolores, who always referred to herself in third person plural, "We are nauseated and dismayed at our daughter's assumption that such a sordid infatuation merits even a hint of our benevolent approval. Our answer to her reckless pleas for our blessing is a firm and generous *no*, for we can't bear the thought of callused hands scratching her delicate skin. Horror of horrors! We shall rather die than allow her royal womb be contaminated by the vulgar seed of a trivial peasant that grinds grain for a living."

Where Dolores saw uncouthness, Esperanza saw beauty. The callused hands of the miller felt like the finest silk when they were dusted with flour, while his seed tasted better than lilac honey, the most refined of sweeteners.

The princess was greatly saddened by her mother's

disapproval and bitterly cried herself to sleep every night. Only her nanny sympathized with her suffering, for she was a simple woman, devoid of pretense and prejudice.

"Sweet child," she said to Esperanza and handed her a handkerchief, so the princess could wipe the dripping boogers from her nose, "you shouldn't turn crying into a habit, for instead of relief, it will only bring you bitterness. There are other men in this world. As years go by and your beauty flourishes, you will attract many dignified suitors."

"Nanny dearest," replied Esperanza, "you have always tried to console me in moments of desperation, but you must know that it is disingenuous to lie just to make people feel better. Unhappiness is best dealt with when it is acknowledged, and my tears are just an expression of my pain. They come from the depths of my heart and shall only cease when it shrivels and dries like a raisin, for love flourishes neither in dignity, nor in the hope that someone else could take the place of the beloved, but in the bliss of complete self-abandonment."

"Sweet child," said the nanny, "the words that I said were a test, for they can only console those who experience mild infatuations, but are powerless against true love. Now that I know for certain that your feelings are not superficial, I shall help you see your beloved again. Tonight, when darkness falls over the palace, I shall let the miller through the kitchen door and lead him right to your bedroom."

"Nanny dearest," said the princess, "how could I ever repay such kindness?"

"It is not gratitude that I seek, sweet child," said the nanny, "but the soothing comfort of seeing two hearts unite, for that is the rarest blessing one could ever hope for. However, you must remember that no matter how delightful your encounter might be, you have to keep silent, for any sound of excitement could alert the guards, and, gossipy as men are, they will certainly denounce you to the queen."

"I shall not let a sigh louder than a gust of breeze escape my mouth," vowed the princess.

The nanny did as promised. That same night, Esperanza and Joy embraced again, to their hearts' delight.

It is said that when lovers are meant for each other, the gods take special care to match all the curves of their bodies, so when they join, they become one, and it is not possible to see when one body ends and another begins. Had anyone peeked through the steamy bedroom window, they would have thought the blurry silhouette on the bed was that of Esperanza alone, tossing and turning in the throes of sadness. Indeed, it often happens that opposite emotions trigger similar reactions in the human body, for crying occurs both in moments of deep despair and great joy. Only observant poets know the difference, for despair paints the eyes red and causes swelling, while joy makes them glitter like emeralds under the brightest of suns.

"Take me," whispered the miller in the ear of the princess, "until there's nothing of me left!"

He thrust into her, caressing her breasts and kissing her neck. Esperanza was overcome by such intense pleasure, she forgot the warning of her nanny.

"Oh Joy, I am yours forever!" shouted the princess in ecstasy.

Like most spiteful people, the queen was a light sleeper and woke up immediately. Angered by her daughter's disobedience and the audacity of the miller, she decided to end their relationship once and for all.

"It is our responsibility as a mother," she said, "to properly educate our inexperienced progeny. We shall punish the princess by withdrawing all desserts from her diet. The peasant—whatever his name was—shall be banished by boat, for he desecrated our noble house, which is an act of high treason."

Since Barbaria was located on a peninsula protruding in the Arctic Ocean, banishment was enforced in two distinct ways, depending on the severity of the crime. People convicted of lesser treason were banished by catapult, hurled over the land frontier to the south. Many of them died from the fall. According to official data, twenty three percent survived without severe injuries.

People who committed high treason weren't that lucky. They were banished by boat in the Arctic Ocean. The freezing currents carried them farther and farther north, where there was nothing but nothingness and no hope for return.

As for her daughter, Dolores needn't have bothered issuing a punishment. The princess lost her appetite anyway, for when one's yearning for love is so brutally suppressed, body and soul quickly wither. Esperanza's fate saddened everyone: rich and poor, young and old. Even innocent babies, who didn't know the pain of a broken heart, cried louder than usual because the milk of their mothers turned sour, tainted by despair.

Before long, the first calls for open disobedience were heard on the streets. Someone scribbled the words *Heartless bitch!* on the wall of the royal palace. The Committee for Social Justice initiated a petition for the immediate

pardon of the miller. A rescue team of the best naviga-
tors sailed in search for him, only to be arrested, moments
before they left territorial waters. The queen sentenced
them to slave labor, despite the pleas for clemency from
the interior ministress herself.

"Common people are free to romanticize taboos," wrote
Dolores in her verdict. "Their lives, unlike those of the
aristocracy, lack a higher purpose. We have always envied
them, just like we envy small children, for they don't
know the burdens of responsibility. We can assure you
that despite the burning anger we feel regarding the des-
ecration of our beloved daughter, the decision to banish
the filthy rascal was taken pragmatically, following the
letter of the law. Any attempt to circumvent it, regardless of motivation, shall be considered an act of rebel-
lion. We benevolently dismiss all appeals and consider
the case closed."

"Down with the evil cunt," someone shouted, while the
ministress of communication read the verdict on the stairs
of the justice department. "Our true queen is called Esperanza and we shall fight to liberate her from this heartless tyranny."

Thus started the biggest uprising in the history of the
queendom. Angry mobs swarmed the streets of the capital.

"We have come to depose the witch or die trying," they
chanted.

Houses were lit on fire. Stores were looted. A group
of radical charlatans hijacked the protest and declared
a republic. Dolores bravely fought the peasants with her
glittering sword and impenetrable armor. Her army was
about to deliver the final blow and crush the uprising
when suddenly, a mighty horn echoed in the air.

When the queen looked at the northern horizon she saw the most unusual sight. An army of iceberg-riding giants was approaching fast.

"Demons of ice," shouted Dolores, "be gone or face my wrath, for once I cleanse my lands from this peasant scum, I shall crush you like grapes!"

The leader of the giants spurred his iceberg. The demonic vehicle jumped out of the water and crashed onto the shore. Its body burst into smithereens that scattered all over the battlefield, trapping the royal army.

"Your sword is useless against me," said the giant. "I am Godwin the Emphatic, emperor of Hyperborea and guardian of the Scepter of Knowledge. For years I have observed you, admiring your perfectionism and pragmatism—qualities that we, the great Hyperboreans, value above everything else. However, when the poor miller arrived to our icy shores naked and shivering like a leaf, and told us how badly you have treated him, I was greatly disappointed. I realized that your severity doesn't come from restrained compassion but from spite and sheer emotional clumsiness. Thus, I have come to end your reign of terror. From this day on, the crown shall grace the head of your daughter, Esperanza, whom I shall immediately marry to her beloved and put an end to this needless suffering once and for all. I sentence you to be their maid and take care of their chamber pots."

And so Esperanza and Joy lived happily ever after until they were visited by death, the parter of companions and destroyer of delights. Glory be to the living gods for only they can judge us!

Interlude: Harnessed Icebergs

"**W**OULD YOU REMIND ME," said the queen to her vizierienne, "For how many years have I ruled this queendom?"

"It's been five years since you ascended to the throne, Your Majesty. May the gods extend your reign as long as possible!"

"Ever since I put this slab of gold on my head," the queen pointed to her crown, "there hasn't been a single moment when I have found my sword useless. In fact, the plating of the handle has completely worn off because there has barely been a week when I don't have to cut someone's head off, and in the meantime I use it to pick up various things."

The queen swung her sword and skillfully lifted the crown off her head. The vizierienne watched it slide down the shiny blade until it hit the bronze handle with a dull clang.

The queen was an excellent swordswoman. She mastered the weapon at the age of eight, when—according to her mother—she could slice a flying butterfly in two. On her fifteenth anniversary, she lined up her thirty six dolls and beheaded them with a single swing, proudly announcing the end of her childhood.

"There is not a problem in this world that cannot be resolved by a sword," said the queen. "It is love that complicates life and makes everyone miserable. Have I told you what happened to the ministress of finance in my mother's cabinet? She worked tirelessly for weeks to pass the annual budget. Then came her husband's birthday.

She loved him far too much to just toss him a gift card, so she went shopping, even though that's not a woman's job. She picked up a beautiful fur coat and headed for the counter. Everyone knew her as an excellent administrator and talented mathematician. Unfortunately, she suffered from directional dyslexia. Instead of paying with her own money, which she always kept in her left pocket, she reached into the right one and used public funds. You can imagine what followed—a scandal, accusations of greed and corruption. A deranged social justice warrior even demanded her execution. Her husband took full responsibility. She did it out of love, he said teary-eyed, if someone should be punished, it should be me. But the same masses that indulged in fairy tales of iceberg riders avenging peasants shouted at the top of their lungs *Lock her up! Lock her up!* They were threatening to storm the palace if my mother showed any sign of clemency. The ministress was sent to jail. Her husband cut the fur coat in pieces and made mittens for thirty homeless orphans. A week later, he hanged himself in front of the tax office. I can live without a coat, he wrote in his suicide note, but without her, I'm nothing."

The queen sighed and put the crown back on her head.

"Love, my dear is the opium of the masses," she continued, "and once people get high on it, they will trample you like wild horses."

"Gods know the crowd has many flaws," replied the vizierienne, "for when people join together, their vices multiply in geometric progression. But we can also find a lot of wisdom in their melodramas because they remind us that life is not only about governing."

"Where you see wisdom, I see immaturity," said the

queen. "The story you just told must have been written by pubescent boys. Only they can dream of something as ridiculous as harnessed icebergs. To think that people are entitled to satisfy the infatuations of the heart is childish. It is unfortunate, of course, that calculating taxes is not as fun as wrestling in the bedroom. Don't get me wrong! I wish the world was different, that all our desires were instantly fulfilled, that we didn't have to suffer loss and disappointment, much less anger or anxiety or loneliness. Alas, the gods reward only those who think pragmatically, while those distracted by emotions are left behind and occasionally executed for treason."

"Your Majesty is right," said the vizierienne, "for love certainly causes confusion. Yet sometimes it is the confusion itself that brings unforeseen fortune."

"Give me a single example and I promise not to cut your head off," said the queen.

And so the vizierienne began another story.

The Enchanted Stew

I HAVE HEARD, oh fortunate queen, that on the other side of the world, there is a country called Patasarriba where everything is upside down and people have the most peculiar customs—they put their carts before their horses and their plows before their oxen. Their days go backwards, from sunset to sunrise. Men are wiser than women, and everyone talks in reverse, which, being the norm, is considered quite natural.

Once upon a time, in those strange lands where nothing was as it seemed, lived two brothers. They were twins, identical in every way. Not even their mother could tell them apart. As babies they cried and slept at the same time, and one would refuse to eat if the other was away. Thus they grew up, sharing everything, and nothing could ever come between them, for they knew neither envy nor jealousy.

This went on until one day they fell in love with the same woman. And because, oh fortunate queen, in those primitive times polygamy was forbidden, and men could still choose whom to marry, the brothers had to decide who would be the lucky one to take her as a wife.

"Dear brother," said the first one, "I wish I could share this woman with you like we shared our mother's milk, but since we cannot split her in two without killing her, I shall claim her solely for myself."

"Why do you think this would be the right thing to do?" asked the other.

"The reason is very simple," replied his brother. "My feelings for her are so intense that my mind knows no rest.

No matter how hard I try, I can't stop thinking about her. I have therefore decided to offer her all my possessions in exchange for her hand."

"I feel exactly the same," replied the other, "and since we inherited an equal amount of wealth from our parents, none of us would have an advantage."

Unable to resolve the impasse on their own, the brothers decided to try out their luck. On the next morning, each one killed a spotted goat and cooked a delicious stew with pickled lemons and lilac garlic, following a recipe they inherited from their grandfather.

Once finished, the brothers went to a nearby hill, where centuries ago a bunch of gossipers had built a shrine. Each put a plate of stew below the statue of a man crucified on a four-leaf clover, which was exactly how the god of serendipity—who was immortal—chose to sacrifice himself for the benefit of humanity. He knew that, according to the first law of thermodynamics, the total happiness in a closed system couldn't be increased from within. Since all deities existed outside the Universe and weren't bound by its laws, the god of serendipity assumed it was possible to tweak the constant through self-inflicted suffering. He incarnated himself into a human egg, lodged in the uterus of an unsuspecting virgin. Once he came of age, he started a disruptive cult that threatened the very foundations of civilized society and brashly challenged the authorities to execute him. He died in horrible agony. To balance things out, the level of internal happiness in the Universe increased to such an unsustainable level that a new force called *chronic dissatisfaction* spontaneously arose from the quantum vacuum to prevent the entire creation from collapsing.

Soon after, the first prayers advanced towards the heavens like a shockwave from a thermonuclear explosion, and all gods became inextricably involved in the pettiest of human affairs.

$\sim\sim\bullet\sim\sim$

"Oh, god of serendipity, who died in our name," said the brothers in one voice, "we have brought you a delicious stew. Let the one who cooked it best win your favor and marry the woman we have both fallen in love with."

The god of serendipity, who was always hungry, immediately came down from the heavens. He ate a spoonful from each plate and pulled on his beard.

"I can't make the slightest difference, but that's probably because I'm always hungry," he said. "Fortunately, my wife, the goddess of missed opportunities, is notoriously picky and doesn't have much appetite, so I shall consult her and get back to you as soon as possible."

The god grabbed the plates and ascended to heaven.

"Try this," he said to his wife, and handed her a spoonful of stew.

"What is it?" asked the goddess of missed opportunities.

"It's the best stew I have ever eaten," said the god of serendipity.

"That doesn't say much," she replied and rolled her eyes. "You would eat demon liver if there's enough barbecue sauce to help it slide down your throat."

Little did she know that the god of serendipity ate demon liver every night, but like many other things, he kept it a secret, for he knew his wife was prone of dismissing everything adventurous.

"I can't understand people's obsession with wine," she said once to her first cousin twice removed, the god of carnivals. "It's nothing but spoilt fruit juice that people used to drink out of necessity because fresh water wasn't readily available."

She was, of course, right in theory. If back in those primitive days drinking water wasn't such a health hazard, nobody would have been experimenting with fermented liquids. Yet it wasn't the relative safety of the mild anti-septic that people found attractive. They drank wine not to quench their thirst, but to lighten their mood.

Demon liver tasted like rotten flesh, but contained a chemical that triggered a throbbing erection. It was a side effect the goddess of missed opportunities immensely enjoyed, although she had no idea what caused it.

"You're right," said the god of serendipity to his wife. "My taste buds are not nearly as sensitive as yours. That's exactly why I need your help."

The goddess of missed opportunities sniffed the spoon and raised an eyebrow.

"Is it spicy?" she asked.

"Absolutely not!" replied her husband.

She cautiously tasted the stew. After a brief pause, during which she carefully assessed her mood—for unbe-knownst to her, it played a big part in the way she per-ceived the world—she nodded approvingly.

"Do you want more?" asked her husband.

"Maybe just another spoonful," she replied.

This time the god of serendipity dipped the spoon in the other stew and handed it to his unsuspecting wife.

"Strange," said the goddess of missed opportunities. "Now that I tried it again, it seems a bit overcooked."

Indeed, while the second brother was cooking, he lost track of time because the sound of the bubbling stew reminded him of the rumbling in his stomach when he lusted after his beloved. As a result, his potatoes became a bit too mushy.

"Whoever cooked it must have been distracted by something," said the goddess of missed opportunities.

"Thank you! That was all I needed to hear," said the god of serendipity and hurried back to the altar, where the brothers patiently waited for his judgment.

"It was a tough call," he told them. "Both meals were exquisite! However, according to my wife, the first one tasted better."

"Thank you, master of providence! I shall worship you and your wife until my dying day," said the first brother and bowed down, barely holding back his tears of joy.

"My wife would be happy to hear that," said the god of serendipity. "She is a woman that's hard to please and rewards only those who always aim to be perfect. However, my job is to look after those she unjustly ignores. You and your brother are equally skilled at cooking. His meal came second because he lost track of time, thinking of his beloved, while you, striving to follow the recipe by the letter, forgot about her."

And thus, against all odds, the second brother married the beautiful girl, while the first remained a bachelor. They lived happily ever after, until they were visited by the parter of companions. Praise be to those who focus on things that truly matter.

Interlude: Of Love and Privilege

"**W**OULD YOU REMIND ME," asked the queen, "what is the greatest duty of a responsible monarch?"

"Of all responsibilities resting on the blessed shoulders of our rulers, the most important one is to treat all subjects justly," replied the vizierienne.

"And what kind of treatment is considered just?" asked the queen.

"A treatment that is morally reciprocal to the deeds of the person subjected to it."

"And what if the queen finds some of her subjects more pleasant than others?"

"In this case, it is advised that the queen doesn't take into account her personal sympathies because in a just society all laws should be applied impartially, as to avoid confusion that could give rise to discontent."

"You are well read in the principles of governing and claim to be knowledgeable on the subject of love. Tell me then, why is such a benevolent force only a privilege of the beautiful? I've never heard a single love story about ugly people," said the queen.

"That's because most storytellers are biased or superficial," replied the vizierienne. "In reality, love can be experienced by everyone, regardless of appearance."

"Then, if you value your life, tell me a story that proves it," said the queen.

The Monstrous Bride

A STORY IS BEING TOLD, o fortunate queen, that once upon a time, in the Queendom of the Briny Lake, there lived a princess that was unusually beautiful. This was all the more surprising, for the harsh climate of this region made all its inhabitants ugly. The constant winds blowing over its salty soil made their skin coarse like sandpaper.

The princess had many suitors—men from all parts of the queendom would come to beg for her hand, but she couldn't make up her mind whom to marry, for she was afraid that people valued her most for her appearance, and not for her personality. Her indecisiveness worried her mother, the queen, because she desperately wanted to have grandchildren.

"You are still young," she said to the princess, "but there will come a time when you will regret your pickiness. People who are too demanding in their youth eventually settle for the worst once their faces wrinkle."

"Oh mother," said the princess, "faces might wrinkle and breasts might sag, for all things made of flesh are prone to decay. Unlike them, the human spirit is incorruptible and everlasting. Those who value it above everything else don't know loss or disappointment. I want a man who will love me for who I am and won't leave me when I turn fifty, just like my father, whom we haven't seen in ages."

"It is typical for the young to use wise words irresponsibly, for they can't match them with experience," said the queen. "Wisdom is like a crown—you can put it on your head and pretend you're a queen, but unless you have a loyal army and a docile government behind you, people will consider you delusional. It is unfortunate that the mistakes of the parents are so easy to spot, while those of the children are yet to be committed, but this is the way of the world, and there is nothing I can do to change it. However, you should know that your words have inflicted pain in my heart. One day you will regret them, but I won't be around to accept your apology. When that time comes, don't waste your time in useless penitence, but remember that I have already forgiven you, because my love for you is bigger than my pride, and there is no pain I wouldn't endure to make your life easier. I'd rather risk provoking your hate than letting you down. Therefore, I must warn you—if you don't pick a husband in three months, I will have no other choice but to do it for you."

It was indeed a custom in those lands for monarchs to pick a spouse for their children and the words of the queen greatly worried the princess, who swiftly sent messengers to all corners of the queendom, inviting all able-bodied men to a dating tournament.

"The winners shall be summoned to my bedroom for further questioning," she announced, "for I must marry a decent man before the leaves turn golden and the weather gets cold."

Thousands gathered below the walls of the royal castle. For three weeks they competed in all disciplines of the trivium and the quadrivium, which at that time consisted of wine tasting, oil wrestling, and mud fighting; as well as bush pruning, sheep shearing, goat milking, and horse riding. It was the beginning of summer, and the days were hot and long. The entire capital stank of sweaty armpits and musky pubes. At the end of the third week, a grand jury of female elders selected three finalists: a knight, a merchant, and a butcher. After a mandatory shower, they were invited to the bedroom of the princess. The queen patiently waited in the hall, overjoyed that her daughter was finally about to marry. Suddenly, the princess stormed out of her bedroom, cursing.

"What happened?" asked the queen.

"Oh mother, you're asking me to do the impossible," said the princess.

"For the sake of all gods and spirits, pick the one and let's get this over with," said the queen.

"You don't understand," said the princess, "I like all of them. They're all perfect, but..."

Her assessment of perfection, of course, should not be taken out of context. It is relatively easy for those with agreeable appearance to stand out in a land where most people look hideous. Nevertheless, the three men were the pinnacle of what could be called *feasible perfection*— something that the princess wasn't quite interested to begin with.

"I like them all but how can I be sure which one loves me the most?" she asked.

"Did they genuflect when they entered your premises in a princely fashion?" asked the queen.

"They did, and each of them lowered a knee all the way to the ground without losing balance," replied the princess.

"Did they pledge their loyalty to you as they gazed upon your cleavage?"

"Most certainly, and they used the exact same words!"

"Did they whisper sweet nothings in your ear?"

"Yes! Their breath was fresher than lilac peppermints."

"Tough choice," said the queen, "Perhaps you need a rest. It was a long day. The morning is wiser than the evening."

The princess went to bed, ridden by anxiety.

"Goddess of love," she prayed as she closed her eyes, "help me pick the one that loves me for who I really am!"

———~~~———

It was Friday. Way up in the heavens, the goddess of love was dining with a bunch of friends. They were just finishing the main course, debating whether to order dessert. A waiter approached, carrying an envelope on a golden plate.

"There's been an express prayer for you ma'am," he said.

The goddess of love winked at him and slapped his buttocks.

"Surprise, surprise! I guess he decided to call her after all," said the goddess of hope to the goddess of despair, whose face was always veiled by disappointment.

The goddess of love read the prayer.

"Ladies, I know that paying attention to my inbox at this time might appear rude, but this seems urgent. I hope you'd excuse me."

"Darling, if this is the secret diet that helps you maintain your gorgeous body, you have to tell me all about it," said the goddess of infidelity.

"Even if it was," replied the goddess of love, "there's zero chance you'd stick to it for more than three days."

Everybody laughed, except the goddess of despair, who had difficulty appreciating irony.

The goddess of love got into her aphrodontus chariot

and rushed to the palace. The princess had just gone to bed. She didn't expect her pleas to be answered. Like most people, she considered prayer a form of soothing meditation. The noise from the landing chariot startled her just when she was drifting off to sleep.

"I know this might seem unbelievable, because I don't answer prayers personally, but your case is tremendously important to me," said the goddess of love to the startled princess. "I'm losing worshipers at an alarming rate. The number of people who believe love is a privilege for a minority of good looking idiots is constantly growing. Since your beauty is quite mediocre and your three candidates are sort of hideous, a widely publicized happy ending would reignite interest in my cult and save my career."

Needless to say it was an offer the princess couldn't refuse.

"There's just one problem," said the goddess of love and moved closer, as if what she was about to say could be overheard by someone else.

"In have to tell you, girl to girl," she continued, whispering, "looks aside, each of these men is a catch! I'm not surprised you couldn't make up your mind, for even I would find it difficult. Rest assured I have a plan, but it comes with one condition. Our meeting should be kept completely off the record. If word about it gets out, I will deny this conversation ever took place and call you a delusional princess that can't make a difference between dreams and reality. Do you understand?"

"No one will ever know," promised the princess.

"Very well," said the goddess of love. "Tomorrow, when the Sun rises, pack a few sandwiches and head to the hills outside the city. There you will see a giant cave."

"I don't believe there's a cave anywhere near them," said the princess.

"There will be one tomorrow," said the goddess of love. "I know a few people in high places that owe me a lot of favors."

"I understand," said the princess.

"All you have to do is get inside the cave and wait," continued the goddess of love. "It's going to take a while. Bring something to read in case you get bored. Eventually, the man who truly deserves your love will come to pick you up."

"Is this all?" asked the princess, "it seems rather easy."

"Of course it will be easy, dear child," said the goddess of love, "you already did your part. While you relax in the cave, I shall appear in front of your men as an old witch and tell them you have been kidnapped by a giant bird that brought you to its cave and is just about to either eat or rape you. I haven't yet decided which is worse. When they hear this, they will rush to your rescue. The one who truly loves you will succeed."

~~~~~~

When morning came, the princess did as she was told and headed to the hills. She easily found the giant cave—there was freshly deposited gravel around the hills and giant footsteps that formed a path leading right to its entrance. Meanwhile, the goddess of love disguised herself as a witch, lest the knight, the merchant, and the butcher see her beautiful face and fall out of love with the rather mediocre-looking princess.

"Distinguished contenders, I have bad news," she said

to them, "last night, a terror bird kidnapped the princess and took her to its nest, which is in a giant cave on the outskirts of the city. Go and save her, for she might be eaten or raped any moment!"

The merchant and the butcher rushed to the cave.

"Oh, shit," said the knight. "I would very much like to do that too, and had I known something like this could happen, I would have brought my shiny armor with me. Alas, I left it back home in my mother's closet. I'm afraid that without it, I could hardly survive a battle with a terror bird. It is most unfortunate that I am unable to help the princess, whom I love so dearly! I swear in the name of the goddess of love that I shall miss her until the end of my days."

"I have never heard a lousier excuse," said the goddess of love, "not to mention how appalled I am by the ease with which you swear in the name of the most noble of all deities."

She struck him with her wand and turned him into a pile of dust.

"There! You shall never speak my name in vain again!" she said.

~~~~~~

The merchant was the first to arrive at the cave. He peeked through the entrance, but saw no trace of the princess.

"Something doesn't add up," he thought. "Terror birds have been extinct for a long time. I have traveled all over the world, but I have never met anyone who had seen one. Even sailors, the most skillful of all liars, don't brag about such encounters. Something else must have dragged the princess into this cave and, judging by the giant footsteps around the entrance, it must have been one of those titans that live on the other side of the world. It is a place I have never been to, but at least I know a handful of sailors who claim to have reached it. Perhaps the cave extends all the way down to those lands, and if I pass through, I could not only save the princess, but also establish a trade route that will make me rich beyond compare!"

As his sight got accustomed to the darkness, he noticed a faint light flickering in the distance.

"Who's there?" he shouted.

"It is I, the princess," said a frail voice. "An evil monster locked me in this cave. Hurry, beloved! Save me before it returns and tears me limb from limb."

The merchant rushed ahead and found the princess chained to a wall. A candle burned right next to her, throwing menacing shadows.

"My love," said the merchant when he saw her face, "even in a state of profound distress you remain the most beautiful woman in the world!"

"Oh, beloved, don't let my beauty distract you in such a crucial moment! Hurry and unchain my hands with the giant key that hangs on the wall next to me," she said.

The merchant did as he was told. Once free, the princess instantly transformed into a terror bird and crushed his skull with her powerful beak.

A moment later, the butcher, slowed down by the heavy meat cleaver that dangled from his waist, finally arrived.

"Damned bird," he shouted, "you have kidnapped the love of my life! Release her, or I shall turn you into a pile of stinky sausages!"

"Hurry, beloved! Unchain me, for the hideous creature

that kidnapped me with its mighty claws will soon return and rape us both," said the voice.

"Mistress of my heart," replied the butcher, "I will honor your request, but know that if this creature returns, I will easily overpower it and craft you a necklace from the claws that dared to scratch your tender buttocks."

"Light of my life," said the voice, "unchain me, so I can feel the warmth of your embrace."

The butcher got close and saw her face.

"Heaven of heavens," he said, "you are more beautiful than ever!"

"Hurry, my dearest," replied the voice. "Don't let my beauty distract you in this crucial moment!"

"I won't," replied the butcher and instead of the key, grabbed the meat cleaver. With a single swing he decapitated the princess. Her head fell down and returned to its true form.

"Despicable monster," said the butcher and spat on it. "Your sweet voice fooled me, but it only took a single look to recognize your cowardly deception! Your disguise was almost perfect, but my true love has a mole on her chin with three silky hairs protruding out of it. The first one is golden like the Sun, the second—silver like the Moon, and the third—black like a starless night."

As he said those words, the cave transformed into a wedding hall. In its middle stood the real princess, dressed in a sparkling wedding gown. Her mole was right where it was supposed to be. Praise be to the living gods, who through trials and tribulations teach us valuable lessons.

Interlude: The Etymology of Love

"TERROR BIRDS were magnificent creatures," said the queen. "Have you ever asked yourself why, despite being extinct for such a long time, people still remember them?"

"No, Your Majesty," replied the vizierienne.

"Then I shall enlighten you," said the queen. "It's all in the name. *Terror* is a strong word. The tongue that utters it trembles like a leaf. In comparison, the word *love* sounds weak and slimy."

"It is true that phonetics can influence the mind," said the vizierienne. "It is far from coincidental that words describing symbols of power often have an abundance of ear-grating consonants. But the origin of the word *love* is quite unusual. It was derived from the name of an ancient Oriental scientist, who laid the foundations of what we now call *medicine*, although most of her works were lost after a tragic accident."

"I love tragic accidents," said the queen, "tell me more!"

The Ballad of Ana Loveless

I T IS LITTLE-KNOWN, if at all, that the word *genius* was invented to describe the boundless intellect of Ana Loveless, the greatest scientist of the Orient. She lived a long time ago, in the darkest of ages, when those lands were ruled by men and the Barren Desert was still dotted by lush oases. Ana rejected the established scientific methods and explored the world with the bold innocence of a child.

"The phenomena that underpin all creation cannot be measured with instruments," she wrote at the age of sixteen in a letter to the chairman of the Oriental Scientific Society. "Nature won't reveal its secrets to those who shy away from it, hidden behind sterile windows. While I greatly appreciate your generous invitation to become a member, I cannot bring myself to accept it, for this would be a betrayal of my most cherished principles. Rest assured that as a fellow scientist, I wish you nothing but success."

Ana was the only daughter of a flamboyant poet and a pedantic engineer—a couple that wasn't meant to be, since people with such opposing personalities found it hard to coexist under a single roof without killing each other. In fact, when she turned seven, her parents divorced.

"Is it my fault?" asked Ana as her father hastily packed his pink-stripe shirts in his crocodile-leather suitcase.

"My innocent child," he said and kissed her forehead, "all evils of the world are caused by adults, whose lives are poisoned by meticulous pragmatism. Your insufferable mother and I are like fire and water and any attempts to reconcile us would only deepen the horrible damage we have done to each other. Please remember that as your parents, we will always be there for you, for although we passionately hate each other and wish we had never met, we care about you more than anything else."

Confused by the answer, Ana went to her mother, who was powdering her face in front of her bedroom mirror.

"Do you know your father likes red lipstick?" she said when she saw her daughter approaching. "That's the only color I've used ever since I met him. I wanted to be his muse. I would have wrapped myself in rags to please him."

A tear rolled down her cheek. She carefully wiped it with a piece of cotton.

"Here's a lesson for you. Never put make up to please someone else," she said and reached for her pink lipstick.

"Mommy, is daddy leaving because he is angry with me?" asked Ana.

"Don't be silly! Not even a jerk like him can be angry at a child for more than five minutes," replied her mother. "Your father is leaving is because I kicked him out. I won't spend the rest of my life with a man who can't keep his pants zipped up. And neither should you. Now go to your room, because it's already past your bedtime."

Her mother often forgot that children weren't well-versed in the art of disparaging metaphors. Ana didn't understand why a zipper was such a point of contention, and unfortunately, she never got the chance to discuss the matter again. Her mother died the next morning.

"They told me she committed suicide," wrote Ana years later. "It was hard for me to accept she was gone. As a child, you imagine death as something ugly and gro-tesque—even unnatural—but my mother looked so serene and beautiful in her coffin, I thought she would wake up any moment. The idea that she could have taken her own life seemed so odd. She was a strong woman and rarely wasted her time in regrets. Looking back, I think it was her broken heart that refused to go on living, not her mind."

Ana grew up under the care of her father's girlfriends, whose names she could barely recall, for they came and went like broom merchants on a flea market. When she turned thirteen, she joined a boarding school, where she felt much more comfortable.

"It seems that growing up brings nothing but confusion," she wrote in her diary. "If my parents were truly as incompatible as they claimed to be, why did they marry each other? And if they were like fire and water, how come such opposite elements coexist so harmoniously in me? I should have long annihilated in a puff of smoke!"

These questions marked the beginning of her life-long interest in *aphrodisiology*—a subject that Ana defined as exploring "the intrinsic irrationality of the human heart." While her body went through the tumultuous metamorphosis of puberty, Ana discovered she was inexplicably attracted by a particular group of people. She enjoyed their company and missed them desperately while they were away. Those people differed in appearance, gender, or intelligence, but every time she laid her eyes on one of them, her cheeks became rosy and warm.

"When people are confronted by a mystery," wrote Ana, "they rush to formulate an answer, so they can get rid of it as soon as possible. And while there's nothing wrong in seeking explanations for things we don't yet understand, our impatience often gets the best of us. We fall prey to simplistic explanations that do us no favors, and we stick to them at great cost, because in our society too much thinking is considered a waste of time. It can be argued which answers are more efficient—those that are quick and incomplete or those that take time to be carefully crafted. Incompleteness inevitably leads to fragmentation, for a clumsy opinion is sooner or later rejected. Therefore, the economy of thought suggests that patient contemplation is more rewarding than hasty deliberations. Mysteries shouldn't trigger anxiety, but exhilaration."

There was, indeed, no shortage of explanations for the strange attraction. Many attributed it to beauty, yet Ana noticed that some of the people she felt attracted to weren't beautiful, especially her co-student Walter. His ears protruded from his head like those of elephants. Her friends found them unsightly and made fun of him. Ana, on the other hand, didn't pay much attention until one day Walter invited her to a picnic in the countryside. They lost track of time, discussing the mating habits of wild rabbits, and finished their last bottle of wine moments before the sunset. As Ana was hypothesizing why male rabbits were sexually dominant, Walter suddenly turned his head and the last rays of the sun hit the cartilage of his ears. Their fluctuating glow—from orange to vermilion—roused a desire Ana had never before experienced. She wanted to caress them, to pass her fingers over every fold, and feel the pulse of his heart through the blood pumping up and down the intricate mesh of their capillaries. No, thought Ana on her way back home, such an attraction had nothing to do with beauty. If she wanted to solve its mystery, she had to look elsewhere. As usual, the first clue came when she least expected.

"Yesterday, Alice—my best friend in the world—suggested we should safeguard our friendship by becoming blood sisters," wrote Ana a week later. "Her ideas always amuse me, so I agreed without hesitation. She reached into her purse and took out a magnificent dagger. She said it was a present to her father from the prince of Cockaigne. Its handle was gold-plated and encrusted with pearls. I was so taken by its beauty that I didn't notice what Alice was telling me until she pressed it on her thumb. A few drops of blood streamed down the blade. She licked it and passed the dagger to me. I felt a bit embarrassed for not paying attention, and—to demonstrate my resolve to participate in the ritual—I grabbed it quite enthusiastically. Suddenly, my hand was dripping with blood. Alice scolded me for ignoring her warnings about the sharpness of the dagger. Her frustration was justified, since my only excuse was that I got distracted by its looks. Anyway, we were relieved to find out the cut wasn't as deep as our initial panic made it seem. Alice suggested I should lick the wound. She said my saliva would help it heal faster. Right then, I had a revelation."

It is indeed quite normal for genius people to experience epiphanies in the strangest of moments. Epidemius of Choleropolis discovered the cure for influenza while running after a thief who stole his wallet. He faced an unpleasant choice: continue the pursuit or rush back for a piece of paper and write down the insight before he could forget it. To the detriment of humankind, he was a greedy and selfish man, so he chose to recover his wallet. Just a few weeks later, Calculania of Pythagorea was strolling in a park when her beloved dog, Actaeon, was attacked by a pack of homeless cats. As she bent to pick up a stone and chase them away, she accidentally discovered the first ever algorithm for factoring rational polynomials. Not allowing her personal sentiments to overshadow her responsibilities as the leading mathematician of her century, she stoically took out a notebook and wrote down her discovery while the berserk felines tore Actaeon into pieces.

"While I licked my own blood," wrote Ana, "I was greatly intrigued by its metallic taste. This uncanny property surely meant that just like iron, blood was susceptible to magnetism. Hence the mysterious attraction was just a manifestation of a hidden force, binding individuals with corresponding polarity."

It was an elegant idea that nevertheless had to be confirmed by experiments. Ana spent the next few years searching for a definite proof. The greatest difficulty was obtaining sufficient amounts of blood, and quite often, she had to use her own. The frequent bloodletting took a toll on her wellbeing, yet nothing could dissuade her from completing her goal.

"Once I demystify the mechanics of romantic infatuation," she wrote, "I will free humankind from a lot of useless suffering. Looking ahead, I see a world where everyone has an equal chance to find a soulmate and divorces are anachronistic artifacts from a barbarous past."

Great pursuits bear unpredictable fruits, says an Oriental proverb. Inadvertently, Ana's research revolutionized medicine. By a process called *sedimentation,* she discovered blood was a complex substance consisting of four essential elements. The first one was *black bile*—a tarlike liquid with low viscosity that was extremely dangerous to handle. Anyone who came in direct contact with its refined form was overcome by anger. The second, *yellow bile,* resembled urine and was an excellent mood enhancer. The third, *white bile,* smelled of onions, and its vapors made people sad and desperate. A glass of the fourth, named *vermilion bile* significantly improved physical strength. Expanding on her research, Ana established that the equilibrium of these four substances had a profound effect on the human character. The blood of soldiers contained high amounts of black bile, while that of chronically sad people was dominated by white bile.

The four biles became known as the *platonic fluids*—named after Ana's cat, Plato, whose behavior was always exemplary. In fact, by analyzing the data from his blood tests, Ana pioneered the method of *character calibration,* through which she helped many emotionally unstable people regain their sanity. Regardless of this monumental achievement, Ana never strayed away from her original goal. Apart from the four platonic fluids, she discovered that blood contained small amounts of impurities that stuck to the glass of the retorts after the distillation process. To remove them, she rinsed her equipment with *aqua regia*—a fuming cocktail of *aqua fortis* and *acidum salis* that, due to its rapidly diminishing potency, had to be prepared immediately before use.

One day, Plato, chasing a mice in the lab, knocked the last jar of *acidum salis* off the table. Startled by the noise, the cat jumped into a plate of potassium permanganate, lost balance, and fell back over the broken jar. The *acidum salis* reacted with his permanganate-dusted fur, and the animal got completely engulfed in poisonous fumes. Two hours later, Plato drew his last breath. His tragic death broke Ana's heart. She mourned the loss of her companion for a whole week, during which her lab remained closed. When she finally returned, she saw the residue had fallen off the walls of the glassware, forming heaps of fine powder at the bottom of each retort. Its original grey color had changed to sparkling lilac. When Ana reached to take a sample, the powder slid towards her fingers, as if pulled by an invisible force. The mystery was finally resolved. The magnetism of the substance was too weak to be detected when it was naturally dissolved in human blood and manifested itself only between individuals with a matching balance of platonic fluids.

"Had my dearest Plato not suffered such a horrendous death," wrote Ana, "I would have never stumbled upon this discovery. He will always have a special place in my heart and I shall never forget him."

Since physics hadn't yet become a science, Ana couldn't have known that, due to entropy, all promises containing the word *never* inevitably decay and break apart. In the passing years, the memory of her beloved pet faded away, and by the time she met her future husband, Alan Loveless, she could hardly recall the color of Plato's fur.

"Words fail me when I think of Alan," wrote Ana on the day she first saw him, "for he is a riddle trapped inside an enigma. Ever since I laid my eyes on him, I feel strangely hopeful, which is most surprising, since I don't believe in destiny or premonitions. The magnetism between us is so strong, I suspect we have an almost identical blood balance. Of course, this is just a frivolous assumption, for I didn't have an opportunity to sample his blood. I briefly considered staging an accident with a broken glass and gently pricking his finger. Alas, such a performance required a great deal of coordination—something I was utterly deprived of in his presence. Whenever he looked at me, my limbs ceased to obey my mind. It was a disturbingly embarrassing, yet profoundly pleasant experience, for my body felt like a feather dancing in the wind."

Ana wondered if the weightlessness of this feeling was just an illusion or there was something more to it.

~~~~~

"Those of you who have been to my lectures know I don't shy away from fringe ideas," said Ana in her commemorative speech at the Institute of Social Engineering, "and I'd like to use this wonderful opportunity to throw some unorthodox ideas in the air, if only to make it less stuffy. I promise you, I'm not going to grade your opinions."

The students laughed.

"Some people ask me what it feels like to have completed my mission in life so early," continued Ana under cheers and applause, "and my answer always disappoints them. Completeness is an illusion. In fact, completeness is the most dangerous illusion of all. I would rather believe in flying horses than dwell in its deceptive comfort. My work is anything but complete, and I doubt it ever will be. It takes a brief stroll through history to see that every resolved mystery is replaced by a new one. There has never been a shortage of unanswered questions about the world, no matter how well we thought we understood it. So, with this in mind, what kind of secrets lie beyond the already discovered principles of human attraction? Well, knowing why you are attracted to someone doesn't automatically explain the physical symptoms you experience: the goosebumps, the dizziness, the lightheaded trance-like state that resembles floating on a cloud. Perhaps one day some of you could discover that this magnetic force interferes with gravity. If we find out how to take advantage of it, we would be on the brink of a much bigger scientific revolution. You would see how easily my name will move from the covers of the textbooks to their footnotes. And I would welcome that, for it would mean we had moved forward as a society, as a culture, and as a civilization."

When Ana finished her speech and saw the admiration in the faces of her public, her heart filled with sadness. If she could trade all this for a drop of Alan's attention, she would have done it in an instant.

"He seems unimpressed," she wrote later that day, "If I weren't an expert, I would have assumed he was immune to magnetism, but I think he's just afraid to face his own vulnerability. I can only imagine the struggle between his mind and his heart."

She decided to give him a little bit of time, so he could adapt to the new reality.

~~~•~~~

"I am convinced more than ever that he is the right man for me," wrote Ana six months later, "for his resolve not to show affection is a testament to the power of his will, and, being an independent person myself, this is among the qualities of character I value most. A man in control of his feelings is a man you can count on in difficult moments. I am more worried about my own resilience, since the magnetism, pleasant as it is, also makes me lethargic. My productivity has plummeted, and there are days when I can hardly bring myself to make a cup of tea, much less continue my experimental work. My favorite pastime, it seems, is to curl up on my sofa and rub my face against my plush pillow, imagining it is Alan's face."

"I wonder when Alan will finally reveal his feelings to me," wrote Ana after another six months had passed. "I am deeply humbled by his efforts to impress me, but my patience is running dangerously thin. Maybe I should have a word with him, just so I can assure him he can confide in me without fear that I would use his secrets against him."

"After a long deliberation," continued Ana a week later, "I decided I should do some preliminary tests. Perhaps there might be some irregularities in his blood? Had the circumstances not been so delicate, I would have openly asked him to participate in the study. Instead, I opted for an innocent deception. I invited him to the lab under the pretext that I needed help with its decoration. We sat down to talk, and I offered him tea. I figured that, being left handed, he would take a sip from the right side of the cup, so I slightly chipped the porcelain at its rim, just enough to scratch his lip and draw a drop of blood. Everything happened as planned. I acted as if I was surprised and apologized profusely. After he left, I rushed to analyze the sample."

The results raised more questions that answers. As Ana expected, the balance of their platonic fluids was similar, but no matter how much she tried, she couldn't detect even a trace of lilac powder in his blood.

"The greatest question science has to answer," wrote Ana, "is not what the world is made of or how it was created, but why the things that make our lives meaningful are inspired by its imperfections. Alan's emotional inertness is clearly caused by the purity of his blood. In my most horrific nightmares, I find myself inhabiting his body, passing through life like a shadowless ghost, serene and unmoved—a spirit devoid of desire, bound to a soul that doesn't know yearning. How many others suffer this fate without knowing?"

A week later, Ana invited Alan for tea again. This time, she served it in an impeccable cup. When Alan took a sip, she saw his face brighten and in the sparkle of his eyes she recognized the flame of desire.

"All it took was a bit of lilac powder in his tea," she wrote, "and he was all over me. I only wished we could remain like this forever."

From then on, she added a spoonful of it every time they met, and they soon married.

~~~~~~

One afternoon, when Ana got back from her lab earlier than usual, she saw a pair of trousers on the floor of the living room. She picked them up and noticed a stain of red lipstick on the zipper. Her heart hollowed out like a wounded piñata. Then, unexpectedly, she finally understood her mother's warning. Instead of heading to the bedroom, where she was certain she would have found Alan in the embrace of their maid, she ran to the cemetery. She didn't believe the dead had the slightest interest in conversing with the living, but she needed to tell her late mother that she learned her lesson, albeit too late.

"Although my aching heart is begging me to join you in death, I have unfinished business in this world," said Ana and kissed the marble gravestone.

Later that night, flames engulfed her lab.

"They say to forgive is divine, but I am not a goddess," wrote Ana in her farewell note.

Overwhelmed by bitterness, she turned away from science and became a powerful sorceress. Her blood spells lured men away for their homes and turned them into slavish marionettes.

Interlude: Pride and Punishment

"**I**'VE HEARD ENOUGH," said the queen. "If I learned anything from these silly melodramas, it is that love is an obsessive compulsive disorder that needs to be cured, not encouraged."

"Your Majesty, if these stories haven't persuaded you of the power of love, the fault must be entirely mine, for I am not a professional storyteller. But I assure you, a simple gesture of kindness towards your people will greatly improve your popularity."

"Kindness?" said the queen. "Am I not kind enough for taking care that everybody abides by the law? My days pass in sentencing criminals and collecting taxes. Do people think I'm enjoying it? That I don't want to run away? Do you know how heavy this crown is?"

"I am sure, Your Majesty, that governing people is the heaviest of burdens," said the vizierienne.

"Forget governing," said the queen angrily, "I'm talking about the crown itself."

The queen pointed to her forehead.

"If you had the faintest idea how uncomfortable it is to balance a piece of metal on your head each day," she said, "you'd be thanking me for my sacrifice instead of preaching empathy."

"I didn't mean any offense, Your Majesty!" replied the vizierienne.

"Too late," said the queen. "I am already offended! I've tolerated your inefficiency for years. Now, apart from useless, you've also become extremely annoying. I sentence you to death."

"Your Majesty, I don't fear death," said the vizierienne and fell on her knees, "but I beg you to spare my life, for I have nothing but your best interest in mind, and I wish to serve you more than anything."

"I might spare your life under one condition," replied the queen. "Admit that all those stories are nothing but gibberish."

"Then my fate is sealed, for I cannot tell a lie to you," replied the vizierienne.

"Perhaps a night in the dungeon will help you reconsider," said the queen and ordered the guards to lock the vizierienne in the darkest prison cell, so she could meditate in peace and come to the right conclusion. When morning came, she was summoned back to the throne room.

"Did you sleep well?" asked the queen.

"I did not sleep, Your Majesty," said the vizierienne.

"How so?"

"At first, it was cold, and I couldn't stop shivering. Fortunately, after an hour, a guard appeared and wrapped me in a woolen blanket. It had your initials woven onto it. As he was warming my hands, he reminded me how merciful you can be to those who don't disappoint you."

"Who knew men could be so insightful. I shall give this guard a promotion, whoever he might be," said the queen.

"Then, as I was drifting away," continued the vizierienne, "a woman in the torture chamber across my cell started screaming. I don't know what unspeakable things the guards did to her, but I heard her bones cracking. She must have vomited several times, for her screams were interrupted by gargling, and her voice became coarse as if someone jammed a sheet of sandpaper in her larynx."

"It must have been the head of police," said the queen. "She conspired with extremists who held an illegal protest against my rule. Fortunately, after she denounced them, I revoked her death sentence and replaced it with life imprisonment. She will spend the rest of her days in luxurious solitary confinement, which is something I myself often fantasize about. I have promised to supply her with ink and paper, so she could write her memoirs and in return she pledged to dedicate them to me," said the queen.

"I could tell her issue was resolved because after about two hours, the screaming stopped and was followed by a dull noise, as if someone was dragging a body across the floor."

"And what kept you from falling asleep after that?" asked the queen.

"Nothing," replied the vizierienne. "Since I knew that in a few hours I would be dead anyway, I preferred to spend my last moments on Earth with my eyes wide open."

"A peaceful death must feel like falling asleep," said the queen. "It's a shame that because of your stubbornness, your end will be much more unpleasant. Hopefully, your execution will be a lesson to those who waste their lives with silly stories."

Many sociologists had tried to explain why common people were so drawn to public executions. The most distinguished among them was Saint Simon de Rouvroy, who spent four decades studying crowds, disguised as a homeless beggar. Minutes before his death, he published his magnum opus, *Studies on Bread and Circuses*. Through the use of differential equations, he proved that, once social cohesion reached a certain threshold, human egos dissolved, and people began to identify as a homogeneous group. He likened the process to bread production, where individual grains of wheat were gradually turned into a mushy paste, and ultimately shaped into a single loaf. Saint Simon successfully demonstrated that the dissolution of the egos prevented people from empathizing with each other. Thus, public executions served as cleansing rituals, since criminals weren't considered individuals, but mere pimples on the face of society that needed to be urgently popped.

~~~~~

The execution of a minor bureaucrat usually attracted about fifty people. That of a senior government official was attended by several hundred, depending on the severity of the crime and the celebrity in charge of reciting the sentence.

When the queen looked at the crowd gathered on the main square, she was delighted to see it was larger than anything she had seen before. Yet the sea of heads was exceptionally calm. Instead of cheers, there was silence. People seemed to even have left their favorite posters at home.

The queen refused to delegate the role of announcer to a mere celebrity. She wanted to send a personal message to anyone who thought she could be swayed by petty emotions. Her booming voice permeated the square, amplified by her diamond-encrusted megaphone:

"Esteemed subjects of all ages! When I became your queen, I took a pledge to serve justice to all, regardless of social status or origin. I have spent my reign trying to fulfill that promise, and thanks to your unconditional support, we are inching ever so closer to a society where all criminals are treated justly. Today, the rich and powerful share common jail cells with the poor and the disadvantaged. The aristocrats are beheaded as easily as the peasants. We've come a long way! Just a century ago low-income criminals comprised ninety eight percent of those sentenced to death. Now their share has fallen to seventy four. Yet before we congratulate ourselves for this tremendous progress, let us remember that equality is not a final destination in a long journey, but a delicate equilibrium between cause and effect, responsibility and consequences. This equilibrium is constantly under threat. On one side, there is the danger of poor judgment, which arises every time we turn our backs to reason and embrace our emotions. On the other, there are hideous conspiracies that intentionally aim to mislead and corrupt us. And sometimes, unfortunately, the enemies of reason hide right next to us, disguised as benevolent friends, caring relatives, or trusted servants. Yesterday, with great sadness I discovered that my vizierienne has been plotting against me. Through the cunning use of storytelling, she tried to dissuade me from sticking to the letter of the law. Look at the people, she told me, they need love and affection more than they need order and discipline! When I heard those insulting words, I was appalled on your behalf, for they implied you were immature and weak, like children."

"No to the nanny state," someone shouted.

"Wise words," said the queen. "Had my vizierienne not lost her sanity, she would have known how futile it was to try to change my mind. She would have refrained from exposing herself as an enemy of the state. Alas, she foolishly assumed my judgment could be swayed. For that, esteemed subjects, she deserves to be punished. However, just as I am, I also believe in second chances. I offered her a path to redemption, if she agreed to repent."

"Everyone deserves a second chance!" someone shouted.

"We are a land of opportunities," said another one.

"Sadly," continued the queen, "she declined to do the right thing, and therefore she will be promptly executed!"

The crowd erupted in rapturous applause.

"Some of you might be asking themselves," continued the queen, "how can this be an execution, if there is no executioner in sight?"

Actually, nobody was in the mood for questions. People were too excited to notice the absence of the hooded woman that executed all convicts. Her name was Esther and she had taken a brief leave only once in her career, just before she gave birth to her daughter. Now that the queen pointed out she was missing, people assumed she gave birth to a second child.

"Who's the father?" someone asked.

"Don't look at me!" another one replied.

The crowd giggled. Three separate rumors regarding her absence emerged spontaneously and spread through the masses with lightning speed.

Esther and the Hyperborean (Take One)

I HAVE HEARD, SAID SOMEONE in the crowd, that a while ago, a great tragedy befell the kingdom of Cynocephalia. A Hyperborean giant arrived to its shores riding an iceberg the size of a castle and wreaked havoc on three coastal towns.

When the news reached King Anubis II, who by the grace of the gods ruled these lands, he sent a legion of soldiers to capture the berserk savage. They ambushed him in a shrubby forest. A great battle ensued and all soldiers died, except a coward, who didn't dare to enter open combat.

"I should thank the gods for my cowardice," he thought as he watched the giant gut his comrades one by one, "for if I were brave, my intestines would have been already wrapped around my neck. It is fairly obvious that strength and size are related, and the only way to beat such a brute is through the cunning use of trickery or magic."

Since he wasn't a magician, he had to rely on *ingenuity*—a quality that cowards possess in spades, for it is essential to their survival in this cruel world. After a bit of head scratching, he invented a sophisticated contraption called a *sling,* and hurled a stone at the giant's head. The glacier-colored eyes of the Hyperborean rolled back, his bulging muscles deflated, and he collapsed unconscious, squashing twenty six corpses under his enormous body. Their blood squirted upwards and stained the thick clouds that covered the atrocity from the sight of the gods, who at the time were celebrating a birthday and didn't want to be disturbed by unpleasant views.

The soldier assembled a platform from broken chariots, tied the giant to it, and dragged him to the capital.

One might think the Cynocephalians—who resembled humans but had heads like dogs—were cruel and vindictive like most animals. Alas, this assumption was not only insulting, but profoundly wrong, for this folk of semi-humans was among the gentlest and noblest of all, and in their kingdom, the rule of law was above everything. The Cynocephalian constitution gave even bloodthirsty aliens a right to legal assistance and consular support.

Since Hyperborea didn't have a consulate in Cynocephalia, King Anubis II ordered his most distinguished diplomats to sail north and establish contact with the Hyperboreans. Everybody knew the mission was doomed, for beyond the Arctic Ocean there was nothing but nothingness. Nevertheless, the diplomats embraced the opportunity to uphold the principles of their homeland. A year after their departure, they were officially declared dead and were interred in the Cynocephalian Hall of Heroes, right next to the victims of the Hyperborean giant.

Sticking to the letter of the law, King Anubis II personally assigned a lawyer to the giant, so his trial could go ahead and he could be sentenced for his crimes. The atrocities he committed were so horrific that during the proceedings half of the jurors developed severe psychological trauma. The counselors that treated them documented thirty seven new types of mental disease. Four of them were collectively declared *Person of the Year* by the Cynocephalian Academy of Science—the highest honor for exceptional contributions to society. After four months of painful deliberations, eyes swollen with tears and nails bitten to the bleed, the jurors completed their deliberations. The savage was declared guilty of premeditated genocide, sexual assault, illegal trespassing, and aggravated hooliganism. Each sentence carried a separate penalty. The first one was hanging, the second—ten years in a high security prison, the third—a fine of ten thousand dinars, and the fourth—public whipping.

Adding them up wasn't easy. If carried out in a descending order of magnitude, the first would cancel the others. The reverse also presented a problem, although not as obvious: People sentenced to public whipping couldn't be simultaneously fined, for the combined humiliation would irreparably damage their self-esteem and thus limit their future contributions to the public good. Additionally, those sentenced to pay a fine larger than one thousand dinars couldn't simultaneously go to jail, for the state was legally obliged to immediately offer them a job, so they could recuperate their funds through hard and honest work. And finally, anyone who could spend ten years in a high security prison was entitled to a fresh start in life because the Cynocephalians believed in redemption.

The Supreme Court deliberated for a month how to resolve this legal conundrum. After half of the judges fainted from exhaustion, the conflicting sentences were replaced with the harshest single punishment permissible by law, originally intended for people who committed matrimonial assassination by sexual witchcraft—the most reviled crime in Cynocephalia. The last person sentenced to it was Hatshepsut IV—a power-hungry queen who killed her husband Thutmose XVII by turning his butt plug into a poisonous snake.

The punishment was called *breaking on the wheel*—a most elaborate type of execution, specifically designed to demonstrate the severity of the Cynocephalian justice system. Those subjected to it rarely survived, for few souls could withstand such crushing anguish.

Firstly, the body of the criminal was anointed with a foul-smelling ointment made of wax and sulfur, while a choir of children performed *The Anthem of the Condemned,* a musical piece with a dreadful melody and a pace known to cause arrhythmia in individuals past the age of sixty. And while a fortunate minority of people found the melody pleasant, nobody could stomach its harrowing lyrics:

> *The glitter of this filthy potion*
> *Shall not blind us to your crimes.*
> *The stench of sulfur will remind us*
> *Of those that died before their time.*
> *For every damage there is retribution—*
> *A prison term or hefty fine,*
> *And in the sacred name of justice,*
> *We shall slowly break your spine!*

After the performance, a young priest lit the *bonfire of justice*—an exorbitantly pompous name for what was a medium-sized candle, placed in a porcelain censer. Its wax slowly dripped over a cup of *lapis vitae*, a non-combustible incense made from the resin of the shepherd tree, whose blossoms, surprisingly, gave birth to lambs. Consumed in small amounts, it had laxative properties, while an essential oil derived from it was used by hairdressers for hair curling. The Cynocephalians were unaware of all this and used it for its scent, which helped neutralize the smell of sulfur. A brief intermission followed, so people could get snacks from the food stalls around the square. The criminal was then placed on a cartwheel with his limbs stretched out. The headsman, wielding *the hammer of justice,* delivered the first blow, breaking the left foot and gradually moving upwards until no leg bone remained intact.

Once done, he started tearing chunks of flesh from the broken limbs with the *pincers of retribution,* while his assistants poured hot tar with ladles called the *spoons of mercy* to seal the wounds. As the criminal deliriously begged the gods for forgiveness and denounced his vicious deeds, the crowds greeted his remorse with encouraging remarks. It was common to see children on the shoulders of their parents. This type of execution was especially recommended for those under the age of twelve, because the gruesome sight was an excellent crime deterrent.

Another intermission followed, so people could relieve themselves in the portable toilets or get a dessert. During executions, the amount of consumed confection increased significantly. Many treats were sold exclusively at these events. The most beloved were the *screaming cannoli*—pastry rolls made of fried dough, shaped like a tube and filled with whipped cream. The name was inspired by the way they were eaten. People slurped the delicious cream and used the funnel as a loudspeaker to shout obscenities at the agonizing victim.

A gong announced the third part of the execution, when the arms of the criminal were subjected to the same procedure that left his legs mangled beyond recognition. He would often pass out from the severe pain and the headsman would announce a short break until the criminal regained full consciousness.

The fourth part began with a priest who recited *the*

prayer of remorse. Finally, the executioner swung *the axe of indulgence* and in one swoop cut off the head of the criminal.

~~~~~~~~

The execution of the Hyperborean giant didn't proceed as expected. A custom cartwheel had to be constructed, since the largest one available barely covered his buttocks. Then, three headsmen took turns, struggling to break a single bone in his body. They gave up one by one, drenched in sweat and gasping for air. Another three tried to rip chunks of flesh with their pincers but only managed to tickle him. And when the time came to decapitate him, their axes shattered like icicles when they hit his neck.

This most unfortunate outcome greatly saddened King Anubis II. Since the foundation of Cynocephalia, all prophets predicted that a failure to serve justice would spell the end of the kingdom.

The king sent a message to all monarchs of the world, pleading for help:

Dear colleagues, I am Anubis II, King of Cynocephalia, a land of order and justice, where no crime is left unpunished. A great tragedy has befallen me and my people, for we have sentenced a criminal to death but none of us can kill him. Every second that he remains unpunished chips away at the foundation of our society and brings us a step closer to imminent collapse. I am humbly asking you to send your most merciless executioners to my capital and help us carry out the sentence to its end.

When the queen of Severia received this message, she summoned Esther, for there wasn't a butcher on this Earth more proficient in the slaughter of sinners.

"Esther," said the queen, "I have a an important job for you."

"Your Majesty," said Esther, "I hope it involves cutting heads, since this is what I excel at."

"It most certainly does, my dear," said the queen. "To the east of our island, there's a kingdom full of dog-headed midgets who can't tell the difference between torture and tickling. Apparently, a Hyperborean rascal landed on their shore and trampled their meadows or something. They sentenced him to death but, being small and pathetic, soon discovered they can't actually kill him. Now their king is freaking out, thinking everything is doomed. Normally, I wouldn't move my finger to help such incompetent abominations, and I would gladly leave them to the mercy of the Almighty Evolution. But there is a political aspect. Suffice to say, an alliance with those midgets might come handy in time of political need. Therefore, I command you to pack your axe, head to this land, execute the idiot, and come back home as quickly as you can because if people find out that my executioner is missing, they will become even more unbearable."

"To hear is to obey," said Esther, "I will depart right away."

Three days later, she arrived in the Cynocephalian capital, greeted by a jubilant crowd.

"Oh, harbinger of justice," said King Anubis II. "We welcome you to our kingdom and hope you'll feel like home among us."

The look of the Cynocephalians bewildered Esther, but

the queen warned her not to comment on their facial features.

"Thank you, Your Majesty and handsome midgets," she answered, "but I am under strict orders to return to Severia as quickly as possible, because my queen needs me. Please take me to the convict who needs a head removal, so I can fulfill my assignment."

Esther might have been prepared for the strange looks of the Cynocephalians, but she was caught off guard by the Hyperborean, who was blissfully sleeping in his prison cell. When his snoring reached Esther's ears, she felt her neck tingle. The feeling was pleasant but confusing, since she usually preferred high-pitched noises. Once she made a man scream continuously for three minutes just by twisting his ankle. It felt so exhilarating, she could hear a choir of heavenly jinns singing.

When Esther entered the cell, she saw the Hyperborean curled up on the floor. His giant back slowly expanded and contracted, following the pace of his breath. I better sharpen my axe well, thought Esther, for I have never seen such a thick and muscular neck in my life.

~~~~~

The sudden surprise brought back memories from her past, when she was still a young apprentice. She used to watch those older than her cut heads with a single blow, while she could barely sever the spinal cord of a malnourished peasant. She remembered the voices of her mangled convicts, choking on their own blood, begging her to deliver a fatal blow. *Kill me already! Kill me already! Swing harder and end my misery, you incompetent cunt!* She remembered the pain those words inflicted upon her, how she clenched her teeth trying to ignore it and act professionally, how she fought to hold back her tears, and how, once they burst through, they stung her eyes and blinded her... And then she would hear her supervisor shout *Stop! Stop! Enough already!* And she would wipe her eyes and look down, where instead of a human head, she would see an ugly heap of minced meat and bone shards. *Squishy Esther*, they called her. *Sausage maker, meat grinder, head popper, brain kneader...* Every new insult scarred her self-esteem, deeper and deeper, until one day she swore to never pick an axe again and become a landscape artist. Yet when she saw that every tree leaf she painted looked like a dagger, she realized she couldn't run away from her destiny. The path to greatness didn't lie in talent, or hard work, but in pristine clarity of one's purpose. She was born to wield blades, not brushes. Once that purpose was revealed to her, Esther felt like a butterfly bursting out of a cocoon. People's ridicule couldn't harm her anymore. From then on, every head she cut could be perfectly identified. Her blows became so swift and precise, the faces of her victims looked serene, as if they died blissfully in their sleep.

She shook her head to clear her thoughts. The neck of the giant was massive, but she knew how to wield an axe and cut the sturdiest muscle as if it was made of butter. It wasn't the size that troubled her, but the unusual appearance of the Hyperborean. His skin was whiter than snow—a complexion she had never seen before. The color of his hair was bright like a carrot, while his arms and shoulders were dotted with spots of glittering ocher. His curly locks were shifting from deep orange to light yellow. Then, there was his smell—delicately sour, like the cream filling of a screaming cannoli. If only she could have one now.

She licked her lips and moved closer. The giant groaned, as if he sensed Esther's presence. She instinctively grabbed her axe. He sighed and turned around to reveal a face glowing like a rising sun. His eyebrows and the stubble on his cheeks had the color of his hair, and his milky-white chest was graced by nipples the size of dinars, pink and spongy, surrounded by tiny strands of golden fur.

Esther let go of her axe. For all the years she spent honing her skills, she had never regretted taking a life. She thought her conscience was clear because she was following orders. Now she realized she was wrong. Despite coming from different walks of life, she and her convicts had many things in common. This made them expendable. Now, in front of her lied a man so unique, she couldn't take her eyes off him. If she decapitated him, she would be agonizing in regret until the rest of her life.

"Your Majesty," she said after she came out of the cell where the Hyperborean was still sleeping, "Do not regret letting this monster live. He is more dangerous than you can imagine. Had you managed to cut his head off, two more would have appeared from its bleeding neck. The only way to kill him is to take him up north, where there is nothing but nothingness, and push him over the Great Abyss, for everything thrown in this bottomless pit perishes forever without a trace."

"We have heard of this place from our forefathers, who were great sailors and reached every corner of the Earth," said King Anubis II. "However, all maps and atlases were recycled for we needed paper to draft the very laws that made our society just and prosperous."

"My queen sent me here to help you in any way I can," replied Esther. "It will be an honor to push this monster from the edge of the world on your behalf, so he won't bother anyone ever again!"

King Anubis II gladly agreed, and Esther sailed away with the Hyperborean. Only the gods know what happened next, for the skies were clear enough for them to observe the shenanigans of this most awkward couple in history. Unfortunately—if Esther's account could be trusted—on the seventh day, a snow storm appeared out of nowhere and the giant fell overboard, while she escaped with minor injuries and some unexpected bouts of what she thought was sea sickness. When she disembarked and the symptoms didn't disappear, she found out she was with child. This happened nine months ago and only a select group of people in the palace knew about it, since Esther's mission was classified as confidential.

Esther and the Hyperborean (Take Two)

BEWARE, COMPATRIOTS, of unfounded rumors! Truth is easily twisted by ignorant minds, tempted by spurious certainties that lie beyond their reach, just like the land called Cynocephalia, of which there is no account anywhere, except in the cavernous wilderness of people's fraught imagination.

It is a well established fact that species cannot interbreed, and any frivolous combination of their respective features is impossible. An elephant can't grow the legs of a gazelle, and a cat's head can't replace that of a donkey, except in our worst nightmares and perverse fantasies.

It is, however, logical to conclude that races of corrupted humans inhabit the extremes of the world, for their unfavorable climate prevents the body from developing harmoniously. By the rules of the Almighty Evolution, these unfortunate conditions produce a plethora of hideous monstrosities. To the west, where the cold winds blow over the steppes, live people whose eyes are hidden in the palms of their hands and whose feet have fingers instead of toes. Down south, where the intense sunlight dries the deepest rivers and water is scarce, live the double-humped tribes. Their body fat accumulates in two cysts on their backs, so they can keep cool in the unbearable heat. The North, where there is nothing but nothingness, remains unexplored, although our most distinguished scientists advise us to keep an open mind. Who knows, the hypothesized existence of the Hyperboreans might turn out to be true, if only some of our absentminded explorers return with a credible story of a serendipitous encounter. There are, indeed, rumors that our most distinguished executioner, Esther, had seen one of those imaginary creatures, but under much different circumstances.

To the east of Severia, our thrice blessed island of plenty, lies a queendom called Epiphagia. It is among the strangest on Earth: people there have no heads, their faces reside on their chest, and their noses protrude from their sternums. They have mouths instead of bellybuttons and eyes instead of nipples. Their grim appearance is not caused by the peculiarity of the climate, for the weather in Epiphagia is pleasant year-round. Rather, it is a consequence of a decadent ideology called *egalitarianism,* which emerged as counteraction to the rabid individualism of the first settlers.

Since the geographic isolation of the Epiphagians limited their cultural exchange with the rest of the world, they held on to this ideology for centuries, as evidenced by the commandment *Thou shall not stick thy head in the crowd!* inscribed on the ancient walls of their parliament. Consequently, people's heads descended into their rib cages and their brains merged with their lungs. The egalitarianism also corrupted their system of government, which from an enlightened oligarchy regressed to unmanageable chaos. They called it *democracy.*

It is alleged by numerous substantiated accounts that recently, a stranger was found on the shores of this queendom, snoring on a beach near a fishing village, three thousand forearms northwest of the capital, Acephalopolis.

He was indeed described as Hyperborean, for the only place he could have come from was the Far North. This assumption was also supported by his strange appearance:

His eyes glittered like sapphires, his lips had the color of pomegranate seeds, and his chalky-white skin was peppered with ocher spots, like satin sheets sprinkled with tea. His chest hair had the color of the setting Sun and was softer than Abharazarhadaradian velvet. His perky nipples looked like rose buds in early spring, while his armpits smelled of fermented milk. His legs were wider than temple columns and he could crush coconuts under his feet.

When she saw him, the Epiphagian queen, Marie Antoinette, was greatly alarmed by the freakish protrusion on his shoulders that hosted his face.

"This poor creature has no doubt developed a tumor that has pushed his facial organs above his chest. Judging from the horrible noise he makes, his brain must be suffocating. It's a miracle he's still alive. Yet before I accept this diagnosis as credible, I shall organize a referendum, so the entire population can have a say about it," said the queen.

It took a day for all the Epiphagians to vote and another one to count the results. Fifty-three percent of the population agreed with her.

"Now that we have diagnosed his sickness, we have to make an effort to cure him," said Marie Antoinette and clapped her hands. "Guards, put him in a cage and feed him some cake until I decide on the best course of action!"

While the guards carried out her orders, she pulled the chief of the intelligence service to a side and whispered in his ear (which was of course located right below his armpit):

"Jacques, darling, remember that a year ago our spies intercepted a message from the Syscephalian ambassador to his agents? He described a similar disease that plagued the Far West and turned people into freaks."

"I certainly do, Your Majesty," replied the intelligence chief, "and I shall immediately send spies to investigate the matter."

~~~~~

Six months after that, the spies returned with a report spanning six thousand pages, distributed in three hundred folders, mounted on the backs of twenty four horses.

"Your Majesty, I have good and bad news. Which one would you like to hear first?" asked the intelligence chief.

"Jacques, darling, if it was up to me, I would definitely prefer to hear the bad news first, for although it might be upsetting, there would still be something good left to cheer me up. Alas, I think this is a matter that calls for another referendum," said Marie Antoinette.

Since referenda could only be held on a Sunday, they had to wait five days before the ballots could open. The results were announced shortly thereafter.

"It turns out people's opinion once again aligns with mine," said Marie Antoinette. "In fact, I have forgotten the last time they voted against any of my proposals. Doesn't this strike you as suspicious, Jacques? Do my subjects fear me?"

"Perish the thought, Your Majesty," replied the intelligence chief. "It's just a sign that our system of government functions as expected."

"That's nice to hear," said Marie Antoinette and clapped her hands. "Guards! I'm about to hear bad news. Bring me some cake, so my blood sugar doesn't drop too low!"

The queen was served a plate of carrot cake and a glass

of cranberry juice. She hastily swallowed a whole piece.

"Jacques, darling, I'm all ears!" she said and took a big gulp of juice.

"We have learned, Your Majesty, that this disease is called a *head,* and it has reached epidemic proportions. Practically everyone in the West is infected by it. People's faces are protruding above their shoulders like periscopes."

"Oh, the humanity!" said Marie Antoinette and shoved the remaining piece of cake in her mouth, "whahd a twewible twhing!"

"Excuse me, Your Majesty?" said the intelligence chief.

The queen swallowed and took another gulp of cranberry juice.

"What a terrible thing," she repeated. "I am devastated! Guards, bring me a slab of marzipan, quickly!"

The guards rushed to the royal kitchen. The sound of clashing pots and pans echoed in the hall.

"Don't forget to dress it with honey," shouted Marie Antoinette and licked the last crumbs of cake off her fingers.

"They always skip that part. Anyway, I shall be brave!" She sighed. "Tell me, Jacques, darling, how contagious is this disease? Would someone who has, let's say, caressed the tender skin of an infected person, or perhaps kissed the lips residing on that abominable protrusion, contract it? And if so, how long has that person left to live? If she were a suzerain of some sort, should she immediately choose a successor? Needless to say, my inquiry is purely hypothetical."

"This is part of the good news," said the intelligence chief. "It seems the disease is not terminal, and none of our spies has contracted it. We were briefly alarmed by a suspicious growth on the ribs of a young operative, but it turned out to be a harmless pimple."

"Oh, cake on a stick, young people are so disgusting," said Marie Antoinette. "Did you pop it?"

"Our best medics drained all the puss," replied the intelligence chief.

The guards appeared with a huge plate of marzipan drenched in honey.

"Guards, would you please explain to me what does a queen need to do, so she can get her comfort food on time? I almost died while you were dragging your feet in that kitchen," said Marie Antoinette. "Shall I presume you wished to see me dead, prostrated on the floor, drowned in my own saliva?"

"Forgive us, Your Majesty! We wish noting but the very best for you," said the guards.

"I hope so. Now that my blood sugar is back to normal thanks to the soothing words of my intelligence chief, you can throw the marzipan out of the balcony and feed the poor," said the queen.

The guards hurried to fulfill her request.

"Jacques, darling, I apologize on their behalf," said Marie Antoinette, "please continue!"

"The best news is there's a treatment for the disease," said the intelligence chief.

"Fabulous!" exclaimed Marie Antoinette and clapped her hands. "Is it a pomade? A lozenge? A suppository? Are there any side effects? How much does it cost? Meringue on a stick, I seem to have developed some sort of sentiment for that poor creature. Wouldn't it be marvelous to see him shed this terrible tumor and regain his true form? I'm sure he must have been quite pleasing to the eyes before he contracted this debilitating malady. Even now his skin remains so soft, and the hair under his armpits glitters like gold! Oh, look at me, rambling so fast my brain got out of breath! I will shush myself with another piece of cake."

"The cure seems to require a more radical intervention," said the intelligence chief. "Last week, a spy informed us that a surgeon called Esther specializes in removing those tumors with a sharp object called an *axe*."

"Esther?" The queen swallowed and licked her fingers. "What an outré name. It should be banned by a plebiscite. Can we find her?"

"We already have, Your Majesty! An intelligence brigade was just dispatched to kidnap her."

A week later, the intelligence brigade delivered a huge black sack labeled *Handle with care!* to the palace. When the guards untied it, they saw Esther in full working uniform, handcuffed and squinting.

"Meringue on a stick," said Marie Antoinette, "she is just as sick as that poor creature."

Shocked by the looks of the Epiphagians, Esther thought she was having a nightmare.

"Where the hell am I?" she shouted.

"What is she saying?" asked the queen.

"We don't know, Your Majesty. People from the West don't speak French," said the intelligence chief.

"They don't?" asked Marie Antoinette, "What other languages are there to be spoken?"

"We are still studying their means of communication,"

replied the intelligence chief, "so far we have determined they rely on a rudimentary set of sounds to express sentiments and assert authority."

"Great, just as I thought I was on a brink of a scientific breakthrough, my hope was taken hostage by a primitive savage," said the queen. "Guards, I need more cake!"

The guards rushed to the kitchen.

"And don't skimp on the cream," shouted the queen.

"Your Majesty," said the intelligence chief, "some of our experts think language might not be essential for human progress. The fact that a simple woman has developed a cure for such a disease supports that hypothesis."

"A noble savage, how interesting," said Marie Antoinette. "But if she found the cure, why is she still sick?"

"I suppose it's a matter of principle, Your Majesty," said the intelligence chief. "Some medics are altruistic and put the needs of other people before their own."

"Young madam," said Marie Antoinette to Esther, "you can't save the world if you don't take care of yourself first. Healers need help as much as the people who rely on them. This disease has torn your face out of your chest and lifted it so high, you could scrape the clouds with your eyebrows. It's amazing you can still breathe properly. Do... you... understand... me?"

To Esther, the queen's speech seemed like purring.

"Who are you and why have you brought me here," she asked.

Esther was kidnapped after a particularly hard day at work. First, she had to execute three women who robbed a jewelry store. Then, just after she sat down to rest her swinging arm, a man convicted of adultery had to be urgently hanged. She returned home late, skipped dinner, put on her pajamas, and lied down to unwind with her favorite book. The nightmare started as she was drifting off to sleep. A hand pressed a wet cloth on her mouth. Her bed started rocking up and down, as if she was on a ship. Some time after that—she couldn't tell how long—she heard grunting and woke up in complete darkness. Someone uncovered her face and here she was, surrounded by these freaks.

Did she die in her sleep? Was this the afterlife? If so, it wasn't as she always imagined it. She never believed all those promises about an idyllic retreat, where virgin men served nectar to virtuous women. It seemed too simplistic. What she expected from the afterlife was peace. She yearned for a quiet place. The gods knew she loved her job, but she always thought that once she died, she could opt for a dignified retirement. She earned it. While she was contemplating her fate, the guards brought in the Hyperborean.

"This poor creature needs your help," said Marie Antoinette, gesticulating, as if the movements of her hands somehow made things easier to understand.

"What do you want from me?" asked Esther.

The queen rolled her eyes and shoved a giant piece of cake in her mouth. To everybody's horror, she started choking and reached for the cranberry juice. The glass was empty. Gasping for air, she grunted at the guards, eyes filled with blood. They ran to the kitchen. The intelligence chief panicked and tapped the queen's back with such force, the cake shot out of her mouth and splashed all over the face of her defense minister, who was standing right in front of her. Marie Antoinette started coughing compulsively.

"Jacques, darling, I owe you my life," she said after her brain finally filled with air.

In the meantime, the guards came in with a jug of fresh cranberry juice.

"Too late! Give it to the poor! And bring Esther's instrument, so she can begin the damned treatment," said Marie Antoinette. "Woman of the West, I command you to remove this virulent tumor from the shoulders of this man. And I warn you that failure is not an option!"

When the guards brought her axe and uncuffed her, Esther finally realized what had happened. To her great relief, this wasn't the afterlife. Obviously, she was kidnapped by freaks who wanted her to do what she had always done. Couldn't all this hassle have been avoided if they had just asked politely?

The Hyperborean, who spent months locked in a cage, struggling on a diet of carrot cake and marzipan, had a different hunch.

"I think they want us to mate," he said to her and winked mischievously.

"I wouldn't call that thinking," replied Esther. "Male heads are incapable of coherent thought. But I've cut enough of them to know that you still need them on your shoulders to survive."

"Jacques, darling," said Marie Antoinette, "I think they are communicating."

"I like your feistiness," said the Hyperborean. "Where I come from, women cover their faces and don't speak unless they are spoken to."

"Then I think you should return there as soon as possible because those freaks want me to cut your head off," replied Esther.

"They are definitely communicating, Your Majesty," said the intelligence chief.

"Why would they want you to do that?" asked the Hyperborean.

"None of them has one," replied Esther, "and they probably consider it a problem."

"They might as well be right. Our philosophers say all problems reside in our heads," said the Hyperborean.

"Then I'm the best problem solver in the world," said Esther. "I behead people for a living."

"Interesting! Did you choose that job yourself?" said the Hyperborean.

"It's a family tradition," asked Esther.

"So your parents chose it for you," said the Hyperborean.

"Jacques, darling, this seems to be taking too long! Why doesn't she just go ahead with the procedure and put an end to his ordeal?" asked Marie Antoinette.

"As far as we know, this is part of the treatment, Your Majesty. My agents say such healings take place in front of large crowds and require a lot of social interaction."

"I see," whispered Marie Antoinette, "but I seem to be getting bored, and boredom makes me hungry. I don't want to shout at the guards right now, so would you be so kind to go to the kitchen and bring me some cake?"

"In my country, executioners are born, not appointed," said Esther. "You can't become one by choice. And if you already are, you're not allowed to do anything else."

"Ah, predestination," said the Hyperborean, "sounds familiar."

"What's your profession?" asked Esther.

"Prince," replied the Hyperborean.

Esther burst in laughter.

"Jacques, darling, things got out of control," said Marie Antoinette. "The poor creature irritated her. Now she will leave it to die in horrible agony. Oh, I can barely watch!"

"We shouldn't intervene, Your Majesty," whispered the intelligence chief. "She's a highly skilled professional. I'm sure she doesn't let her personal feelings affect her work."

"You're the first person who finds my profession funny," said the Hyperborean.

"So how did a prince end up with these headless freaks? Did your mother marry you to their princess?"

Now it was the Hyperborean's turn to laugh.

"See, Your Majesty, this unpleasant noise seems to be part of their language," said the intelligence chief to the queen.

"How appalling," replied Marie Antoinette. "Remind me to assign them a French tutor once this is over."

"My father wanted me to marry my cousin," said the Hyperborean. "Actually, I shouldn't say wanted, because he didn't have desires of his own. Everything that came out of his mouth had the word *state* in it: *The state expects you to master mathematics, Kenneth!* Sometimes he even managed to repeat it in a single sentence: *Your decisions should always take into account the state of the state, Kenneth.* He would point to his crown, as if the entire nation was squatting on his head. It made him look like a marionette. He wore what people wanted him to wear, ate what they want him to eat. Meanwhile, he pretended he was in charge, while they pulled all his strings, playing powerless victims and avoiding all responsibility."

"Maybe I should cut off your head after all," said Esther. "You definitely think too much."

"You won't," said the Hyperborean. "I bet you don't even lift your axe without a pile of stamped documents."

It took much more than that. She needed six different certificates, singed by a judge and approved by the Commission for State Sanctioned Decapitation and the Department of Torture. Her inventory was inspected twice a year—from the thinnest ropes to the heaviest chains. All equipment that came in contact with open wounds had to be sterile because the idiots in the health ministry thought even the dead had the right to avoid infections. Esther often worried that if those bureaucrats were left unopposed, one day beheadings would take place behind closed doors, away from the eyes of the public.

"It's hard to avoid thinking when everything around you is fundamentally flawed," said the Hyperborean, "and now I realize that running away isn't a solution either."

"You ran away?" said Esther.

"Not literally," replied the Hyperborean. "I just went for a walk with a bottle of whiskey. Gulp by gulp, I realized I was less and less interested in going back. By the time I emptied the bottle, I decided to throw myself off a cliff. We have a saying: when you drink a lot, your wishes come true. I heard the ice cracking and when I looked down, I saw the ground beneath my feet split in two. A giant precipice emerged, just a step away. It felt very inviting. It's now or never, I thought, and everything turned black. I must have passed out on an iceberg and floated away in the ocean because I woke up on a beach, surrounded by these people. I thought they would sacrifice me to their gods, but it turns out they actually want to help me. So sweet! I wish normal people were half as compassionate as those idiots."

"You're spoiled and gullible," said Esther. "There's nothing more dangerous than compassionate idiots. If you want to get out of here alive, you better follow my instructions to the letter."

"Since I sobered up, I'm not that keen on dying, but the thought of going back home makes me want to drink again," said the Hyperborean.

"That's not your only option," said Esther, "although I must warn you, the world out there is not safe for a beautiful man wandering alone. You'll be lucky to walk a mile without being raped."

"Then cut off my head and let's get it over with," said the Hyperborean.

"You know I can't do that," said Esther. "If a word of this gets out, I'll lose my license."

"Even if you do it out of mercy?" asked the Hyperborean.

"Especially if I do it out of mercy. Would you trust an executioner with a heart?" said Esther.

"So what options do I have?" asked the Hyperborean.

"Become my apprentice," said Esther. "Nobody would dare to touch you. Most people won't even dare to talk to you because they think it brings bad luck. There are some downsides. You won't be able to marry anyone but another executioner. It could be challenging if you fall in love with the wrong person, but you toughen up with age."

"What does an apprentice do? Sharpen your axe?" asked the Hyperborean.

"Swipe the floors. Take care of the paperwork. After a year or two, if you're good at it, I'll let you practice with coconuts. In five you'll be ready to cut off human heads."

"And how can we get away?" asked the Hyperborean.

"The crowd is a mindless beast—all we need to distract it is a bit of food and some entertainment. We're quite lucky because everyone seems pretty well fed, so what's left is to put on a good show. I thought a prince would know that better than I do."

"I must have slept through that lesson in governing. But I took a ballet classes. Would that be useful?" asked the Hyperborean.

"Only for children. Grownups are best entertained by torture," said Esther.

"Will it hurt?" asked the Hyperborean.

"Not more than it needs to," she said, "I won't break your bones, but I have to squeeze a genuine cry out of you. Crowds can sniff out fake pain from miles and we can't take that risk."

Since Esther swore she won't utter a single word about what happened next, lest she harmed the dignity of the captive prince, there is no account of the ending of this story. A full description of the event was preserved in the Royal Epiphagian Library, filed under the title *Alternative Medicine: The Effects of Butt Slaps on Facial Deformations*. It was, quite sadly, written in French—a language no one has been able to decipher. Blessed be the gods, from whom nothing can remain hidden!

Epilogue: Love Triumphs and Someone Dies

"**E**STHER IS DOING FINE and she is definitely not with child," said the queen and killed a third rumor, right before it was about to crawl out of the mouth of a desperate houseman, whose life was so dull, he had to invent outrageous stories to make it worth living.

"I asked her to take the day off," continued the queen, "because my vizierienne deserves to die by my own hand!"

She lifted her sword. The crowd went wild.

"Long live our queen!" someone shouted.

"Death to traitors," said another.

"So without further ado, let our celebration of justice commence," said the queen.

A guard brought the chained vizierienne to the scaffold.

It is believed that the only thing that prevents the recognition of economics as an exact science is the so-called *frittata paradox*. Named after a peasant dish made with eggs and vegetables, it posits that during events involving public shaming, a crowd of more than a hundred hungry people will spontaneously generate enough food to feed itself, but immediately waste it by throwing it at the designated target of humiliation. Every economist who has tried to explain this unsettling phenomenon has failed miserably.

The culinary bacchanalia began immediately after the guards removed the hood from the vizierienne's head: A double-yolk egg crashed on her forehead, a tomato exploded all over her white shirt, a zucchini hit her shoulder, and an eggplant landed on her stomach, followed by a ball of wrapped spinach leaves. A ball of cabbage missed

her and hit the guard in the crotch. He screamed in pain and threw it back into the crowd, knocking off a woman who was just about to launch a large pumpkin. In less than a minute, there was enough food on the scaffold to feed a dozen starving orphans for a week.

"Save your provisions, esteemed subjects," said the queen. The irrational frenzy immediately ceased, as if her words broke a spell. Once sober, people tried to recover some of the wasted food, but the guards pushed them back.

"This is a land of opportunity," said the queen triumphantly. "And to prove it, I am going to make an exception. I shall once more urge this traitor, who not long ago served as my trusted vizierienne, to repent and denounce her wrongful convictions. Let us hope she won't waste this chance, for it will most certainly be her last."

"Beg for you life!" someone shouted.

"Crawl for mercy, miserable bitch," said another one.

"Speak before I decapitate you with my diamond-encrusted sword," said the queen.

"Your Majesty," replied the vizierienne, "I have served you in life and, if need be, I shall serve you in death, for I am yours to do as you please. I do not fear death just like I do not fear you!"

The crowd gasped.

"Did you hear her?" asked the queen. "She doesn't even have the decency to fear me!"

"My lack of fear doesn't come from pride or arrogance," said the vizierienne. "I don't fear you because I love you."

The crowd gasped again. An elderly woman screamed and fainted.

"You are not only my queen," continued the vizierienne.

"You are the sovereign of my heart and the mistress of my soul. Just like a sword cannot cut the hand that wields it, I cannot betray or lie to you, for that would mean betraying and lying to myself. My stories were honest and true. All I wanted was to convince you of the power of love, the same one that overwhelms my heart and leaves no room in it for any other feeling, be it the fear of death or the bitterness of disappointment. It is because of love that I surrender to you, completely!"

"You have said enough, vicious succubus!" shouted the queen and lifted her sword. The head of the vizierienne flew off her shoulders like a frightened dove and landed in the middle of the crowd.

"Let this be a lesson to you all," said the queen. "Anyone who doesn't fear my power is a traitor and deserves to die."

She expected cheers and jubilation, but the echo of her words faded in dreadful silence. The queen looked at the faces of the people and saw them covered in tears. Before she could scold them for being too emotional, a rumble bubbled from the spot where the vizierienne's head had fallen, followed by a choir of voices. As they grew louder, the cacophony slowly coalesced into a brief, yet terrifying sentence: *Death to the Queen*, chanted the crowd. Suddenly, an event similar to the frittata paradox took place, yet instead of food, the crowd spontaneously produced pitchforks.

"What a monster!" someone shouted.

"Kill the heartless cunt!" said another.

The queen felt fear for the first time in her life. It was also her last, for merely a heartbeat after, the crowd rose up like a giant wave and tore her to pieces. Thus, the queendom she once ruled with her diamond-encrusted regalia turned into a most serene republic. Blessed be the everlasting gods, for they know better than to mess with love.

The Ebbs and Flows
of the Great Hyperborean Empire

Humble Beginnings

EOPLE FROM THE EXTREME NORTH were considered misanthropic and coldhearted—a stereotype as persistent as the ice that covered their homes. They lived on an archipelago of islands scattered in the frozen waters of the Arctic Ocean—a most bizarre circumstance, especially in the eyes of those who didn't believe in serendipity and second chances.

According to ancient hearsay, the archipelago was originally inhabited by a race of furry cyclops who, blinded by hubris and misguided pride, rebelled against the Goddess of Eternal Ice. For six days they tested her patience. Each time she took pity on them, for she knew they were naturally shortsighted, since they had only a single eye to rely on. But when on the seventh day they brashly threatened to depose her, she felt such burning anger that her icy hair melted. The fit left her bald and unattractive to gods and men alike, and as she wept in despair, the cyclops heard a terrifying noise coming from the sky. When they looked up, they saw her divine wrath descending in the shape of an egg. Its surface was glossy and black, and there were tiny wings attached to its sides. Suddenly, a massive blast evaporated the glacier. The earth beneath it turned into a hot stew and trembled violently. The terrible explosion left a gaping paraboloidal crater. In its middle stood a giant protrusion, surrounded by two rings of petrified cycloptic leftovers—bone shards, weapons, cutlery, and fine jewelry (if, of course, the word *fine* was appropriate for objects meant to fit on fingers thicker than human fists). Shortly thereafter, another crucial accident took place on a small rocky islet that lied on the opposite side of the Arctic Ocean, right off the coast of Trondheim. A corrupt prison guard helped a group of criminals on death row to sneak out of their cells. They swiftly took over the entire prison, dismantled its wooden gates, and built improvised rafts, on which they sailed into the ocean. Upon receiving the news of their escape, the governor of Trondheim province issued the following statement:

My thoughts and prayers are with all prison personnel affected by the traumatic event. This reckless act was committed by hopeless criminals, who were intentionally segregated from our society in the name of public safety. Their escape into the ocean will result in a much more tragic demise than the taxpayer-funded humane method of hanging we provide to all qualifying offenders.

Freezing on a raft was indeed an unpleasantly slow way to die. Many preferred to jump overboard and get eaten by unicorns—marine mammals with an insatiable appetite for human flesh. Had the criminals been even remotely rational, they would have indeed chosen to die on a rope. Alas, those who committed hideous crimes in cold blood were rarely known for their good sense. Back then, even destiny behaved recklessly—idiots were often rewarded with a peculiar blessing called *luck*. The criminals were rescued by a ship stocked with Clonfertian virgins. They were on their way to a summer camp at a nearby monastery, where they were supposed to master the art of knitting sweaters for their future husbands. Many skeptics doubted this chain of events was caused by pure luck. They suggested everything happened because, terrified by the prospect of spending their summer vacation in a monastery, the virgins passionately prayed to be kidnapped by a horde of well-endowed virile men, devoid of shame and sexual inhibitions. These speculations gained credibility, when soon after the accident, a letter in a bottle was washed ashore. It said:

Oh, crescent Moon, master of the waves and lord of all winds! Lead me to a far away place where no one would judge me as I scream in delight while a man berserk with wanton lust ravages my insides with his procreational appendage.

The criminals effortlessly overpowered the male crew and threw them overboard. A flock of unicorns immediately rose up from the pitch dark ocean depths. The sea monsters harpooned the bodies of the unfortunate men with their razor-sharp horns and tossed them in the air like rag dolls. The freezing waters turned into a boiling soup of torn limbs and spilled intestines. Deafening screams soared high as the tortured souls of the victims escaped one by one and headed to the heavens, where even the most misanthropic deities took pity on them and forgave their sins without much bureaucratic hassle.

The criminals were impressed by the viciousness of the unicorns. Their cruelty humbled even Robert the Impaler, who at the age of seven elevated matricide to an art form. He split his mother into three hundred parts, fashioned a baby crib out of them, and donated it to a museum. The clueless curators titled the gruesome artwork *Shelter,* while the critics celebrated it as *a heartfelt expression of exorbitant empathy*.

The macabre feast aroused the criminals. They turned their eyes to the virgins, who lied unconscious on the deck, overwhelmed by the sight of the gory carnage. Only Siobhan O'Giddy stood on her feet, for she used to work in a slaughterhouse since the age of six.

"Filthy pigs," she shouted, "come feast on the nectar of my flower, for by the laws of The Almighty Evolution savage brutes beget the healthiest progeny!"

Thus, the criminals impregnated the virgins and bravely sailed north, hoping to discover uninhabited lands and start new lives, unburdened by karma and social expectations. For nine months they zigzagged through the icebergs until they reached the cycloptic archipelago. Recognizing the strategic position of the crater, they built twelve igloos on the protrusion in its middle, which they called *Storkhome*. Years passed. As the population of Storkhome grew, so did the size of its igloos, until one day their roofs collapsed because of primitive engineering. But then—praise be to all things frozen—an inventor whose name was quickly forgotten found a way to carve tall cylinders out of glacier ice. When erected, they looked like slender tree trunks and could support much heavier roofs. As a result, the igloos transformed into towering cathedrals and the small town of Storkhome became the capital of a mighty state. Its influence spread far and wide over the frozen horizon—a resounding example that political power is achieved not by excessive military spending, but by peaceful scientific exploration.

Magnae Matres

TWO CENTURIES LATER, on the day of summer solstice, when the brazen sunlight turned the thick ice into deadly slush, a young priestess performed the Ritual of Frosted Defiance and slit the throat of a sacrificial mermaid. As she recited a prayer to the Goddess of Ice, the blood gushing out of the mermaid's neck changed color from red to lilac and a strange scent filled the air. Before the priestess could decipher the omen, all men fell on their knees and declared allegiance to her:

Oh, divine mistress! Your gaze holds our eyes captive. Your words delight our ears. We prostrate our bodies before you and beg you to accept our eternal servitude!

The priestess assumed the title of a queen under the name Helen the Gorgeous. Throughout her reign she amassed exorbitant amount of wealth and introduced the institution of *marriage*, so her descendants would enjoy the same privileges that she so effortlessly acquired. Thus, the orgiastic egalitarianism of the early state was replaced by moral elitism. Shortly thereafter, Helen addressed the nation, praising the role of men in society:

"No female deed, big or small, would be possible without our loving fathers, brothers, and sons. It is in them that we seek and find inspiration, for they are the source of all human life. Their groins hold the seed of creation, which through the bond of marriage they so generously share with all of us."

Helen paused to have a sip of water.

"This is a woman's world," she continued to rapturous applause, "for it was built by the hands of our foremothers. Yet such a world would be worth nothing without a man or a boy at our side."

Helen was much less gracious in private, when she felt unrestrained by formal etiquette.

"The only thing men are good for," she once said to her secretary, "is to serve as semen dispensers, just as the Goddess intended. It is therefore advisable not to burden them with too many responsibilities, for their minds are superficial and easily distracted by thoughts of procreation."

The two conflicting points became the foundation of the matriarchal system. Praised in public and denigrated in private, men lived in a state of perpetual confusion.

Helen married her husband, Athelstan the Fecund, at a lavish ceremony, spending half of the state budget. When her advisor told her she should donate her wedding gifts to a public museum as a form of payback, she graciously extended her hand to him and asked:

"Do you happen to have a coin handy, my dear?"

"Yes, ma'am," said the advisor, whose pockets were rarely empty because he never shied away from accepting bribes.

He handed her one made of pure gold. The queen dropped it down her cleavage.

"It fits perfectly, doesn't it?" she said, smiling.

"Indeed, it does, ma'am," agreed the advisor.

"Good," said the queen, "Now take my wedding dress and put it on."

"Your Majesty, I couldn't possibly..." said the advisor.

"You couldn't possibly what? Put it on without tearing it apart because you're twice as large as I am?"

"I'm afraid so, ma'am," said the advisor.

"Herein lies a lesson for you, my dear!" said the queen. "Money is a commodity. Wedding gifts are personal."

The advisor nodded and bowed down.

"Usually, I'm counting on your head to provide the insights," said the queen. "It is your most important asset. If I suddenly decide you have lost your wits, it might accidentally fall off your shoulders."

She kissed his forehead. The advisor held his breath, swallowing nervously.

"Now go and get a rest!" said the queen and retreated to her bedroom, where her husband was snoring.

<hr>

Female supremacy began to unravel during the tragic reign of Birgit the Assertive—an obsessive-compulsive somnambulist, who shouted orders to her servants even while she was sleepwalking. Birgit was the last member of a dynasty that traced its origins way back to Helen the Gorgeous and her twenty one cousins. As if to prove their divine origin, their genealogical tree grew in reverse: Instead of expanding like that of normal families, it progressively contracted, as its branches fused due to institutional incest inspired by entitlement and greed.

Being the last offshoot of an endangered dynasty, Birgit was faced with a dilemma. To ensure the continuation of the line, she had to marry, yet there were no available relatives. After a brief constitutional crisis and a few legislative tweaks, she married herself.

Her son, Albert the Diffident, was as handsome as a prince could be, but his intelligence was somewhat lacking.

Obsessively overprotective, Birgit refused to delegate any responsibilities to him, and he grew up unaware of the meaning of the word *decision*. He declined to eat anything else but his mother's milk. After he turned twenty, his grandfather, Edmund the Disappointed, tricked him to have a candy bar. Albert fell sick, vomiting compulsively for three days. Increasingly paranoid, Birgit accused Edmond of poisoning the prince and promptly executed him.

~~~~~

A day before Albert's fiftieth birthday, Birgit the Assertive rose up in her sleep and headed to the royal kitchen for a scheduled inspection. Distracted by a dream in which a handsome man, vaguely resembling her son, swept her off her feet and carried her to a bed of roses, she accidentally slipped and dived headlong into the birthday cake, where she tragically suffocated. It took four men to pull out her swollen body out of the deadly confection. The mouth of the matriarch, jammed with caramel ice cream, was so grotesquely misshapen, she had to be buried in a closed casket.

Devastated by the sudden loss of his only source of milk, Albert committed suicide. It was the first decision he took in his life, as evident by his farewell letter:

Dearest subjects, as you know I was cruelly abandoned by the person I loved the most. In the early hours of my fiftieth birthday, in complete disregard for my emotional and nutritional needs, my mother left this world forever. I haven't eaten ever since. The sense of betrayal prevents me from sucking the nipples of other women. This morning I was forced to taste something called sandwich that left me disgusted and demoralized. Therefore, I have decided to starve myself to death. Goodbye forever!

Albert's death inspired other victims of matriarchal oppression to come forward and sparked a kingdom-wide movement called *Down with the bosom!* At first its members demanded equal social standing, but an extremely vocal minority of young males, caught up in the euphoria of their sudden emancipation, quickly adopted an aggressive ideology. They believed the female obsession with control was neither a social, nor a cultural construct:

"Women are seductive and dominant by nature, for they have to compete for male attention and retain it," wrote their leader in his manifesto. "It is naive to expect these natural instincts could be voluntarily reined in. The only sensible way to avoid a relapse into matriarchy is to bring all females under the control of men, who—may I be forgiven for stating the obvious—are naturally meek, peace-loving, and emotionally accommodating."

Thus began the *Age of Patriarchy*. Like all other abrupt changes in history, it had a rough start. Many scientific achievements were declared useless and even wrong, for they were developed under a system that actively diminished the male mind.

The Taming of the Shrew

A FTER A DOZEN UNEVENTFUL CENTURIES, during which women gradually learned how to take care of the household, and men spent their time catching up intellectually, a mathematical genius called Gregor the Pedantic ascended to the throne.

Gregor introduced several innovations that revolutionized his kingdom. The first one was the calendar.

"It appears to me," wrote the king in his diary, "that we often quarrel about our history. This is hardly surprising— our recollection of the past is subjective and we always disagree about when and where events took place."

The king was right. There were as many versions of the past as there were people—an unfortunate thing that made any objective study of history impossible. Only the bravest individuals dared to pursue a career in it, enduring incessant mistreatment and abuse. Hardly a day passed without someone being punched in a heated argument. Most historians lost half of their molars before the age of thirty. The frontal teeth of those who studied extremely controversial topics were completely missing. According to linguists, the original word for *history* back then was *thrristhorry*. It morphed into its modern version because no professional could pronounce it properly.

Since historians chose their profession freely and signed release forms before they even started studying, Gregor the Pedantic didn't object to their bullying. But the king detested the chaos that marred the discipline as a whole. How could he leave a lasting legacy if future generations were free to question his achievements, regardless of the facts? Surely, he could outlaw criticism while he was still in power, but there was no guarantee his successor would maintain the same policy. He decided to address the problem at its root—before anything else, people needed a universal system to measure the passage of time, completely independent from any temporal power, even from the sovereign himself.

"I have invented a tool called *calendar,*" wrote Gregor, "that will standardize time for all of us, regardless of age, gender, sexual orientation, or culinary preferences. Time shall be measured in strictly defined units called *years.* Each year shall consist of twelve months, each month— of four weeks, and each week—of seven days. As nature doesn't always conform to mathematical precision, some adjustments might be necessary. I reserve the right to add an extra day once in a while, should any pressing circumstances call for it. Rest assured such additions will be carefully deliberated and won't exceed nineteen per year, except on leap years, when that limit would be extended by one day. Naturally, people born on it will live four times longer than the rest of us."

Ironically, future historians would ascribe a deeper meaning to the numbers of months and weeks. Some would even assume the king thought twelve, four, and seven were sacred numbers. There's little doubt that had Gregor been alive at the time those preposterous theories began to spread, he would have been profusely annoyed.

"Every year shall be named after a different animal," continued Gregor. "There will be the Year of the Mermaid, the Sloth, the Squirrel, the Elephant, the Dogfish, the Fishdog, the Hydra, the Rhino, the Bat, and the Minks. Ten consecutive years shall be grouped in a unit called a *decade*. The decades shall be defined by the adjectives Newborn, Walking, Talking, Pubescent, Adult, Promiscuous, Settled, Mature, Aging, and Geriatric. Ten consecutive decades shall form a century and each century shall carry an emotional modifier—Happy, Cheerful, Delighted, Smiling, Indifferent, Serious, Frustrated, Resentful, Vengeful, and Forlorn. So without further ado, I announce the beginning of the Year of the Happy Newborn Mermaid!"

While Gregor's calendar freed historians from the perils of subjectivity, his second innovation addressed the rampant eroticism that plagued society on all levels.

"It appears to me," wrote the king, "that despite their emancipation, men are still easily distracted by the charms of women. I have calculated that bureaucratic efficiency diminishes by twenty three percent when a woman is present at a government meeting. It further decreases by another twenty seven percent if the woman is smiling, and if she is scantily dressed, productivity grinds to a halt. I believe a similar dynamic can be observed in other aspects of life. To address this pressing issue, I shall introduce a new form of etiquette that would not only ban women from government service, but will require them to cover their bodies in public—from the rosy toes that deliciously adorn their soft feet, to the velvet calves that graciously rest on our shoulders in times of intimate union. Women should also cover their silky thighs, their woolly vaginae, their alabaster stomachs, their rubbery nipples and the dotted circular rims of their pitch-dark areolae. Furthermore, their necks shall also remain hidden, for

there is no other part of the female body that is so vul-
nerable and inviting for kisses, except the cherry lips
that blossom on their faces like fragrant rosebuds yearning to be sniffed. Women shall only reveal their beauty
to their husbands, their fathers, their fathers-in-law, the
fathers of their fathers-in-law (if any of them are alive
and don't have a heart condition), their sons, the sons of
their husbands from other wives (including illegitimate
bastards who live within the household disguised as servants), their siblings and their corresponding male progeny. Women shall also be allowed to reveal their beauty
to small children whose minds are still immune to the
wicked effects of nakedness, and to men who are cas-
trated (either by an unfortunate accident or for purposes
of domestic security)."

Gregor's third innovation was the introduction of free
compulsory education.

"It appears to me," wrote the king, "that our curiosity
and willingness to learn new things is a constant source
of anxiety. Our youth can barely find the time for recre-
ational activities."

It was indeed obvious that people were constantly intim-
idated by uncertainties. They spent too much energy analyzing what was true and what wasn't, relying solely on
their own judgment. After brief but fruitful deliberation,
Gregor concluded that A) learning had to be restricted to
designated periods of the day called *school hours,* followed
by mandatory rests, during which thinking of any sort
was discouraged; and B) learning had to be structured in

a standardized program called *curriculum*—a compound term, formed from the Old Hyperborean words *currum,* meaning *knowledge* and *culum,* meaning *sphincter.*

"We have always assumed the best way to learn that fire is dangerous is to stick a finger in its flames," continued Gregor. "Although effective, this method is extremely dangerous. Hardly a week passes by without a drunk teenager getting fully roasted in search of practical knowledge that could otherwise be safely transmitted by verbal or written communication. To optimize its acquisition, I have invented a device called a *textbook.* Additionally, I am introducing a concept called *common sense*—which states that there are truths equally valid for all members of society. Everyone shall be obliged to recognize those truths automatically and shall never question them."

The Rise of an Empire

ARTHUR THE SERENDIPITOUS, the firstborn son of Gregor the Pedantic, was crowned in the Year of the Happy Pubescent Minks and set the record for the longest ruling monarch in history. He was a passionate philosopher with a penchant for physical exercise. His father raised him to be as benevolent as a human could be, and indeed, both as a thinker and as a ruler, he could do no wrong. Arthur's athletic skills were even more impressive.

One morning, while he was warming up for a run, climbing up and down the inner ring of the crater, he saw a shiny cylinder sticking out from the cycloptic remains.

"Bring this blinging object to me," he said to his servants with a voice that was both authoritative and loving.

They rushed to fulfill the order, but no matter how hard they tried, the cylinder remained stuck.

"Mother of petrified snowflakes," said the king with a voice that was both scolding and compassionate, "do I have to do everything myself?"

Arthur rolled up his sleeves, wrapped his manly hands around the shaft of the cylinder and extracted it with a single tug.

His servants were greatly impressed by his power.

As Arthur studied the object, he noticed that both ends were capped with a transparent material that was clearer than ice, yet didn't melt by the touch of the tongue. Desperate to figure out its purpose, he concluded multiple tests, hitting and pocking his servants with it until one day he brought its lower end to his eye. Immediately, the space before him collapsed, as if his spirit was transported forwards—a most unusual experience he called a *vision quest.* The cylinder, it seemed, allowed him to observe people from afar.

The knowledge he amassed during such observations soon increased his political power and, like a molding lobster, Arthur shed the restraining title of a king and adopted a more fitting one—*eternal emperor.*

The title didn't age well, since he eventually got sick and died in the Year of the Cheerful Newborn Sloth. A day after his funeral, his eldest son, who came into possession of the cylinder—by that time known as the *Scepter of Knowledge*—began exhibiting the same qualities his father was famous for. With the epithet *eternal* removed, the imperial title became hereditary, as did the possession of the instrument. With its help, future rulers steadily expanded the size of the empire. The most famous among them, William the Conquerer, discovered the *Island of the Blessed* while having breakfast on the balcony of his royal watchtower. He proclaimed it a crown dependency right before he bit into his unicorn ham sandwich. A second royal gaze during a cocktail break at dusk turned the island into an autonomous province.

The Fall of an Empire

THOSE OF US acquainted with the intricate life of empires know that no matter how powerful they grow to be—and how indispensable their influence seems to their dominions—there comes a moment when they suddenly fall, like ripe fruits from a tall tree.

The Age of Discovery, ushered by Arthur the Serendipitous, abruptly ended in the Year of the Delighted Geriatric Minks, one day after William's ninetieth birthday. The old emperor woke up, put on his slippers, and climbed up the spiral staircase of the royal watchtower with the agility of a polar antelope. As usual, his breakfast was served on a silver platter, right next to the tripod with the Scepter of Knowledge. The emperor took a bite from the unicorn sandwich and began his daily reconnaissance.

The first look didn't reveal anything surprising. On the streets of the capital life went on as usual. Plenty of polar sloths floated in the sea—half-asleep, half-hungry, waiting for a startled seagull to drop a fish right in their half-open mouths. A bit farther, a flock of mermaids sunbathed on the floating ice. A young unicorn was circling nearby, not yet aware that the flesh of the mermaids stank of benthivorous fish, and no creature would dare to bite them, except the arctic wasp—a small insect whose noisy flight could wake up a drunk soldier from the deepest postcoital dream. The sting of this parasite wasn't a defensive weapon, but an organ for procreation. With it, the wasp injected its eggs directly into the mermaid's bloodstream. Once hatched, the larvae attached to the walls of the creature's heart and gorged on its blood, turning its color from red to lilac. Shamans used the flesh of infected mermaids to brew a potion called *burundanga*. It could subdue the will of the most stubborn people. Ah, thought the emperor, how delightful was this unapologetic complexity! It is not mystery that truly bewildered us, but the things we already knew, for everything was interconnected in pristine hierarchy and its intricacies were unfathomable even to the brightest minds! Who needed new discoveries when there were so many known things to contemplate!

He wasn't the first emperor with symptoms of discovery fatigue. In fact, near the end of his reign Arthur himself found the task of exploration tiring and had to be consoled by an anonymous prophet, who predicted that one day there would be nothing new to discover and all creation would ascend to a higher state of sublime harmony. Like all religious doctrines, it seemed too good to be true, which was exactly why it survived through the ages.

William finished his sandwich, wiped the crumbs off his beard, and somewhat reluctantly turned the scepter to the horizon. It was time for him to fulfill his daily duties.

There was nothing new to the east. He rubbed his eyes, yawned, and turned to the south. The rays of the morning Sun were skimming over the icebergs. Many of them had names because William loved to anthropomorphize objects. It helped him catalogue them more efficiently. While his predecessors used long descriptions like *middle-sized chunk of ice with an ultramarine base*, William just wrote *Wilma* and kept the details in his head. Today he saw Wilma bumping into Björn, a smaller iceberg with a smooth, rounded top. They looked like they were going to remain together for quite some time because the ocean current carried them to a nearby bay, formed by a landslide that happened a year ago. It killed a fisherman and a mermaid. He couldn't remember the fisherman's name, but was pretty sure the mermaid was called Agneta. He missed her. She was beautiful. Once, as she was resting on her back in the water, he took her nipples for faraway islands. He was about to record their coordinates when the mermaid abruptly turned and gave him a severe bout of motion sickness. Nothing of the sort happened today. The South was as familiar as always. Perhaps his eyesight was failing him? If that were true, how come he could see the things he had already discovered so clearly? It was equally unlikely he was becoming senile, for he could still marvel at the world with such pristine clarity. William turned to the west, hoping to end those doubts once and for all. There wasn't anything new there either. Pointing the scepter to the north was useless, for no one had ever done such a ridiculous thing—it was the place where the world ended, and the waters of the ocean fell into the Great Abyss, a truly unpleasant place even to think of, much less to investigate.

It was at that moment when a daring thought pierced his mind: There was nothing left to discover! He was the emperor from the prophecy, the one chosen to complete the monumental task started by his legendary predecessor. He rushed down the stairs, eager to deliver the good news to his government, when his robe got stuck on the parapet. He stumbled and fell. Everything turned black.

When he came back to his senses, he found his body still buzzing with excitement, as if a pack of polar bees had invaded his insides. His muscles were jittering, his heart—racing, his eyes—insatiably hopping from object to object. Light was oozing from the window above his

head. The air was glowing, as if the aurora had taken refuge in the watchtower. The parapet that his hands instinctively latched on felt refreshingly cold. Oh, how foolish of him to rush! Would there be any difference if he announced the news now or waited for an hour? Discovering there was nothing else to discover was the ultimate achievement one could ever hope for. It carried a sense of finality that made time irrelevant. For once William wasn't thinking about the future. It felt like someone just lifted a blindfold off his eyes. Ah, the world was complete! And so was he! And then, inadvertently, the intense feeling turned into a death wish—for just like complete disillusionment, absolute satisfaction diminishes one's will to live. Isn't it strange, he thought, that we think of life as a force of nature, as an instinct independent of the mind, while in fact, what truly keeps us going is the fear of missing out, of passing away before we get the chance to conquer our ignorance!

He heard footsteps. His mind was too self-absorbed to inquire where they came from. By the time his guards reached him, he was thoroughly entranced by a sense of profound gratitude.

"Your Majesty, are you hurt?" a voice said.

"No, child," replied William with a smile.

Anxious panting permeated the calm air. More guards arrived—mouths gasping, bodies drenched in sweat, lungs beating like war drums. Oh, the vitality of youth!

"His Majesty is hurt!" someone said.

William reached for the blurry face of the guard kneeling next to him and ran his wrinkled hand on his smooth cheek—so delicate, unscarred by experience.

"Dear child, you don't understand," said William. The

cheek suddenly turned moist, like melting snow. The guard was crying.

"I am not hurt," continued William, "I am blessed, for I have…"

"Call a doctor!" someone shouted. A cacophony of anxious voices quickly reached crescendo as his words echoed inside the watchtower.

"I have discovered everyth…" said the emperor and died mid-sentence. The complete phrase was nevertheless chiseled as an epitaph on his tombstone.

His opulent funeral was attended by all his subjects, although—due to heavy snowfall—the majority of them were present only in spirit. The first to speak was the minister of royal funerals:

"As we say goodbye to our beloved sovereign, our hearts are filled with sorrow. Yet I compel all of you…"

His throat, dehydrated by sadness, failed him and he paused to take a sip of water. The brief respite allowed people to scrape the frozen tears off their cheeks.

"I dare you!" he continued as his raspy voice regained its strength. "I dare you to rejoice in consolation, for William the Conqueror fulfilled the daunting task set by our first emperor and revealed to us the world in all its glory! He restlessly pointed the Scepter of Knowledge at every cave and iceberg and scraped all mystery off the horizon. His benevolent power spread all over the world like a soft blanked over a sleeping damsel. Never again shall we wander with fear of the unknown, for everything that might appear new shall be something we had carelessly forgotten!"

Blood and Decadence

THREE MONTHS after William's death, his son was crowned as Harold the Disconsolate, by the grace of the Goddess, forever August, emperor of the Arctic; King of the frozen islands, Archduke of the icebergs with perky peaks, Duke of the partially molten icebergs, Prince of all the other icebergs that cannot be easily classified; Landgrave of the Great Abyss and the Island of the Blessed, Margrave of the Cycloptic Crater, Mayor of Storkhome, President of the Royal Household, Object of Adoration, and Subject to None—the last being his preferred title in person-to-person interactions.

By tradition, Harold was raised to be insatiably curios.

"It is my duty as a father to ensure that my progeny exceeds me in all aspects of life," William once said to his son, "for this is how human civilization progresses from barbaric gratification to enlightened dissatisfaction."

"Oh, Subject to None," said one day Harold's minister of health, "I see you pensive and withdrawn."

The emperor was squinting through the Scepter of Knowledge.

"It is indeed crystal clear that my mood has severely deteriorated, although I am looking for ways to improve it," said the emperor. "Do you see that tiny red spot over there?"

Harold pointed to the edge of the moat below the royal palace.

"This is a sight reserved for your eyes only, Subject to None," replied the minister of health.

"Of course," said Harold. "Only an emperor can use the Scepter of Knowledge."

He tapped the looking glass as if it was a pet.

"Of all the rules we have," he continued, "this one makes the least sense. Do you have an idea why the use of the Scepter of Knowledge is restricted to me?"

"Your Majesty, according to the..." The minister of health began reciting the constitution.

"That's not what I asked," interrupted Harold. "Our laws didn't fall from the sky. They were written by men like you and me. Do you know what all men have in common?"

"The desire to serve the state," answered the minister of health.

"Mermaid shitting on glacier," cursed Harold. "Drop the protocol and save us some time! The only thing all men have in common is an agenda!"

Sweating profusely, the minister of health wiped his palms on his robe.

"And what could that agenda be, I hear you ask," continued Harold, even though the minister didn't dare to utter a word, because A) he knew it was time for the usual didactic monologue, and B) he had already seen the red dot the emperor was referring to up close. It was a disturbing sight.

"You see, there are usually three distinct answers, but only one of them is right," continued Harold, delighted to play teacher to someone who was twice his age. "An idealist would say all we want is love. It sounds so pretty! And also petty, because it discards hate, which is equally powerful. Cynics, on the other hand, are much more attuned to the intricacies of life. They would say what we all want is wealth. It's an ugly assumption and no less petty. Wealth is useless without a cause and all causes are by definition abstract. The truth is that the material world is too poor to satisfy our yearnings. This is how we end up with so many dysfunctional rich people. My minister of statistics would have gladly confirmed my words, if he were still alive. He worked tirelessly to improve the mental condition of our wealthiest citizens, whose psychological problems were constantly dismissed as arrogant nonsense. It's easy for the less fortunate to criticize the rich for being unhappy. As if happiness can be stacked on a shelf or exchanged as currency. We often idealize the poor, but let me tell you, material and intellectual poverty often go hand in hand. And then comes a tiny minority of people, those, who for the lack of a better word we call *realists*. They know the right answer. Deep inside, what we truly want, is order. It's how we protect ourselves, our loved ones, our possessions, even our aspirations. Order is achieved through laws that balance ideals and instincts. When that balance is disrupted, society becomes inert and decadent."

Had there been a third person it the room, he would have concluded that the minister of health was listening very carefully. But under the polished facade of attentiveness, his mind was actually busy crafting a praise adequate to the length of the emperor's monologue. When his instincts indicated that Harold's philosophical tirade came to a close, the minister nodded and hunched his back as a sign of respect.

"Second to None," he replied, "my ears are not worthy of so much wisdom. Had I been contemplating for a year,

I wouldn't have succeeded in describing the meaning of life in such succinct manner."

"So," continued the emperor, "now that we agree that laws are subjective, I invite you to break them. Come, take a look through the Scepter of Knowledge, and tell me what you see down there."

The emperor pointed to the red spot again. The minister of health nervously stepped forward. Although he knew what lied down there, he feared to admit it. The appearance of the red spot had alarmed the entire government, or more precisely, its members who were still alive.

"Second to None, now that you mentioned it, I most definitely see it, even without the aid of the scepter," he said, "And I am curious to know what it is, since just an hour ago, the snow below was as white as your honorable teeth."

"It might be hard for you to guess from such a distance, but I happen to know its exact nature. It is the body of the minister of theater."

"Mother of snowflakes! Did he do something wrong?" asked the minister of health.

"No," said the emperor, "but he didn't do anything right either, and you know how much I detest inefficiency. So I commanded him to throw himself from the terrace and he fulfilled my request."

The emperor was lying. Sure enough, the minister attempted to fulfill the wish of his sovereign. However, at the last moment, his hand instinctively grabbed the parapet and refused to let go, even though he struggled to convince it to comply. It was up to the emperor to help loosen its grip by stepping on it until the dramatist fell to his demise, leaving behind a family of two pubescent sons, a daughter, a cheating wife, five dogs, and thirty seven plays, half of them bestsellers.

"Sometimes I think people enjoy dying more than I enjoy sentencing them to death," said the emperor.

"Perhaps Your Majesty will find relief in letting some of them live," said the minister of health.

"What use could there be of a life without a purpose?" replied Harold. "Look at us! Ever since my father discovered everything, we're bouncing off the walls of this castle like headless chicken. It's not only academics who lost their jobs. We all did. That old goat robbed us of everything and conveniently died before he could face the consequences."

"He gave us the knowledge of everything, Second to None!"

"He was a deranged narcissist," shouted Harold.

The abrupt anger startled the minister of health.

"Sweet mother of snowflakes," continued Harold, imitating his father's voice, "I just realized I discovered everything. How could this be! Ah, let me ponder this wonder while I trip on the staircase. Oh dear, I must have fallen in the arms of death! The odds of such coincidence bemuse my enlightened mind. Ah, I shan't be bitter, for destiny couldn't have chosen a better moment for my ultimate demise. And now that I don't have to worry I'd have to deal with a world suffocated by perpetual boredom, I can peacefully ascend to the heavens!"

Harold was so taken by his performance that in the end, he found himself lying on the floor, eyes closed. Strange, he thought, as he was impersonating his father, he came suspiciously close to experiencing the completeness he was so resentfully mocking. If the old emperor could see him now, he would be the one laughing.

"Your Majesty shouldn't exhaust himself with thoughts about the past," said the minster of health. He reached to help Harold get back on his feet.

"Are you one of those people who doubt my stamina or, even worse, my competence to rule?" asked the emperor. "If so, I command you to follow your colleague and jump to your death."

The heart of the minister of health was racing. Ending his life wasn't on his to do list for the day.

"Unless," continued Harold, "you are willing to follow my orders. I just devised a plan to restore society to its former glory."

"Second to None, this is—and always will be—what I strive for. It will be an honor to take part in such a plan, whatever the cost."

"Don't worry, it's easy," said Harold. "Then again, the minister of theater said the same thing before I lost my patience. I commanded him to write a play, one that could free the people from the burden of knowledge. A subversive narrative was all I needed. One that implied all those ultimate discoveries were a scam—a conspiracy—secretly hatched by the government to distract people from their real problems. Do you know what he said? He looked me right in the face with his moist, grayish eyes and told me that to him, truth was dearer than the well-being of society."

"Truth," replied the minister of health, "could be difficult to handle."

"Exactly!" said the emperor. "You see, truth is like medicine—too little will keep you sick, too much will kill you. Isn't this a wonderful metaphor?"

"It's a brilliant thought," said the minster of health.

"Hence I command you to invent a psychoactive medicine that can induce mild paranoia among the populace and restore the healthy sense of mystery that we all enjoyed before my father robbed us from it," said Henry and smiled, waiting for the minister to match his excitement.

After a moment of confusion, the minister of health smiled as widely as he could.

"I will, of course, start research immediately," he replied.

"Excellent!" said Harold.

"In the meantime, could I suggest that Your Majesty takes a much needed break?" said the minster. "There is a lot resting on your shoulders, and a brief nap would certainly energize you."

"You are right," replied Harold. "I need a rest. Do you carry one of your sleep potions with you?"

"I never leave my laboratory without it," said the minster of health and handed Harold a flask full of dark lilac liquid.

The emperor dismissed the minister and retreated to his chambers, where he remained until the end of his life—an event that happened half an hour later.

The minister of health had laced the sleep potion with a poison so powerful, it could kill a herd of unicorns. It was a painful decision. He had been present at Harold's birth and had watched him grow. Yet, as a public servant, his ultimate loyalty lied with the state, not the individual that personified it.

Harold's son, Edgar, was crowned in the Year of the Smiling Walking Elephant. Immediately after the ceremony, the minister of health resigned and, haunted by the moral relativity of his act, committed suicide. Neither his name, nor his achievement was remembered, for unpleasant truths are rarely acknowledged in the annals of history, lest they diminish the impossible ideas we all live by.

A Flare of Populism

HAD PEOPLE TURNED the entire world upside down, they wouldn't have found a more fitting opposite to Harold than his firstborn son. Edgar the Meek, by the grace of the Goddess, forever August, emperor of everywhere, was so considerate and courteous, there were rumors he was a bastard. In his coronation speech, he addressed those erroneous claims upfront, with a hand firmly placed on his heart.

"There are those who say children inherit the sins of their fathers, but I beg to differ. We are best judged not by the expectations that are forced upon us, but by our deeds, which are the fruits of our decisions. As your monarch, I pledge to you that my eyes and ears shall always be wide open, and I shall consult you as frequently as possible, so no decision of mine could cause even the slightest discomfort, or—Goddess forbid—some sort of regrettable pain. I am, and forever will be, your most dedicated servant."

Twenty days after he uttered those words, Edgar the Meek abdicated.

"After a long and exhausting consultation with my cabinet regarding the annual budget of our thriving empire, I came to the unpleasant conclusion that I couldn't, in good conscience, continue to perform the role of emperor. Due to conflicting demands from my ministers, it became obvious that no decision of mine would make everyone happy. Looking back at the pledge that I made, I can't help but think it was a bit naive from me to assume I was capable of meeting everyone's expectations equally. On one hand, there are far too many people in our empire. On the other, half of them is always tempted to disagree with the other half, with little respect for logic or pragmatism. Had I known all this, I would have sworn to rule as a dictator, so I wouldn't have to listen anybody's petty complaints. Before you start whining how disappointed you are by my decision, take a moment to consider how pissed off I must feel to voluntarily give up the best paid job in this empire and how tempting it is to renege on my generous promises. Nevertheless, I stand by my belief that a public pledge should be honored, for if it isn't, people would lose confidence in our political system and the pillars of our society would be corroded by cynicism."

Needless to say, the abdication wasn't an impulsive act. Edgar spent a considerable amount of time in contemplative prayer, asking the Goddess for guidance. Unfortunately, during the entire period of the budget impasse, she was busy with far more pressing matters, and Edgar's pleas were put on hold. By the time she got the chance to examine them, his son, Brandon, was already crowned.

Emancipation

BRANDON THE FLACCID, by the grace of the Goddess, forever August, emperor of everywhere, fulfilled all expectations one could have of a member of a decadent royal dynasty. He was a chaotic administrator and an avid womanizer—qualities that blended well, for one fed off the other like a flame gorging on candle wax. He shared neither his grandfather's obsession with political power, nor his father's reluctance to exercise it unilaterally. To him, the matters of the state were merely a distraction from the transient pleasures of life, and he was known for preferring the company of women to that of his ministers.

"Isn't it amazing," Brandon once said to his minister of philosophy, "that every time an eloquent government official opens his mouth to speak, I feel compelled to yawn, while the simplest sigh coming out of the mouth of my concubines gives me a delightful boner?"

"This is hardly surprising, Your Majesty," replied the minister. "In this world the pleasures of the flesh are easier to appreciate. Yet without the restraints of the spirit to balance them, society would disintegrate under the yoke of sensual barbarism."

Balancing opposites wasn't among Brandon's talents, especially when it concerned things as elusive as the human spirit. His lack of sophistication often infuriated his government, but charmed the common people, who just like him didn't pay much attention to abstractions.

Brandon's first act as an emperor was to order the dismounting of the Scepter of Knowledge—a challenging operation that took a whole week to complete, because the last person who knew exactly how to do it died long time ago, and the instructions he left were somewhat confusing.

The instrument was put in a museum, along with various memorabilia, like the mittens Arthur wore when he pulled it out of the cycloptic remains and the silver platter on which William's breakfast was served each morning. Like most museums, it was only visited by children, forcefully brought there by their teachers.

The royal watchtower was closed for repairs. There were rumors it would be ultimately demolished to make way for a luxurious high-rise igloo that would host various departments of the newly created *Ministry of Entertainment*.

~~~~~

Since there was nothing left to discover, Brandon had a lot of free time—something that made his ministers anxious. They were convinced his grandfather's madness was caused by unhinged boredom. To avoid another bout of irrational violence, the ministers struggled to keep the new emperor busy by expanding his responsibilities. Brandon's breakfast took two hours and began with a ritual called *The Breaking of the Loaf*. Each morning, the best bread in the kingdom was delivered to the palace, so the emperor could slice it with his imperial saber. The bread was then given to the poor as a sign of royal generosity. It was a noble act that nevertheless skewed Brandon's perception of reality, for it implied that A) he was somehow involved in the process of bread making, and B) that a single loaf cut in two could feed all the clerks that lost their jobs on the Day of Ultimate Discovery. Brandon's lunch took three hours and finished with another ritual called *The Blessing of the Blanket*. Every day the best weavers in the kingdom sent their most exquisite fabrics to the palace. After close inspection, the emperor picked the softest and took a refreshing nap called *siesta*, during which he blissfully snored (and sometimes farted), while his royal bowels worked hard to digest the food jammed inside them. Subsequently, the blanket was donated to the poor. It was another noble act that cemented Brandon's misperception of reality, for it implied that A) his body had extraordinary blessing powers, and B) that a single blanket could warm up all the teachers that lost their jobs when it became clear no new clerks were needed to update the royal catalog. Brandon skipped dinner and preferred to spend his evenings in the company of his concubines. It was a controversial habit because A) since the times of Gregor the Pedantic women were considered intellectually inferior to men, and B) men were expected to converse with them only for the purposes of procreation. His ministers didn't object because what happened after working hours was a private matter. They were wrong.

On the first morning of the Year of the Smiling Walking Hydra, Brandon arrived to a government meeting with a severe hangover, wearing nothing but a wrinkled shirt, stained with lipstick.

"I am sick and tired of being a hypocrite," he declared. "In our society, women have been unjustly oppressed for ages and we have to put an end to it."

Nervous rumble filled the conference hall. Most of it was unintelligible, although one could occasionally distinguish words like *travesty* and *effeminate* bubbling through an avalanche of coughs. Ever since the reign of Harold the Disconsolate, cabinet members refrained from open disagreement with the monarch. The short temper of the deranged emperor forced his chief of staff to severely restrict the manner of bureaucratic expression:

In rare cases when the sovereign's ideas seem inadequate and/or ludicrous, members of the cabinet shall express criticism indirectly through mild coughing, during which their mouths should be covered by their right fists. Once the expression of disapproval is finalized, officials should promptly hydrate their throats, as to avoid extra coughs, spontaneously caused by phlegm residue. In force majeure circumstances members of the cabinet are allowed a single clockwise eye roll, performed with a slight tilt of the neck and pursing of the lips.

The coughing gradually died out and was replaced by loud gulps of water.

"Some of you might think I've gone mad," said the emperor and tugged on his lower lip.

A strand of curly hair stuck on it was bothering him ever since he woke up with the legs of the aforementioned concubine wrapped around his neck.

"It's true that women wield enormous power over men, for it takes a single look into their wanton eyes to weaken the knees of the bravest among us."

"Indeed," agreed the cabinet ministers.

"However, blaming them for our weaknesses is irresponsible. What we should do is muster the courage to resist their charms."

"Impossible," shouted the minister of education.

The rest of the cabinet wholeheartedly agreed.

"Allow me to demonstrate," said Brandon and clapped his hands.

A veiled figure entered the room. Although covered from head to toe, several ministers got breathless just from hearing her footsteps. Only one woman could walk like this—the first imperial concubine, Sklud. The Hyperborean gossip chroniclers called her *the temptress of saints*.

She stopped in front of the imperial throne and turned her back at the conference table, facing Brandon. He nodded. She unveiled her face. Brandon remained calm, with a serene, child-like smile.

"This is a trickery," someone shouted. "He's wearing a mask!"

Brandon expected that much. Centuries of institutionalized prejudice couldn't be overcome that easily. He nodded again and Sklud untied her shirt. The skin of her naked back glittered under the candlelight and forced a wave of spontaneous moans out of the aroused ministers. Brandon, who was facing her bare breasts, silently stood up and dropped his pants. His penis was perfectly flaccid.

"If you were still able to speak," said the emperor to his stunned ministers, "you would have asked me whether I possessed some supernatural strength, so I could avoid an instant erection in front of the most attractive woman that has ever lived. Rest assured, the answer is trivial. Once I stopped treating women as pleasure toys and accepted them as individuals, I became resistant to their beauty. Nothing can dampen the urges of the flesh more effectively than intellectual interaction. Once we are aware that—apart from vaginae and breasts—women also have hearts and minds, they become far less attractive."

Thus ended the Age of Patriarchy and everyone lived

happily until, six hundred and forty three months later, in the Year of the Smiling Settled Minks, a ship appeared on the frozen horizon.

A Matter of Size

THEY SAY HISTORY IS MADE by great individuals, but anyone who has ever studied it knows that's just an excuse, so the masses can absolve themselves from responsibility. Historical narratives, just like flesh and spirit, are born from chaos and sooner or later descend back into it. However, since every rule has an exception, it should be noted that there was indeed one person who singlehandedly affected the course of history. Her name was Bartholomea of the Desert—the first woman who traveled the world from end to end.

Born and raised in a desert tribe, Bartholomea was expected to follow in the footsteps of her people, whose main occupation was ambushing caravans and looting oases. Alas, instead of a sense of belonging, the sandy terrain inspired only boredom in her heart. As soon as she learned to ride a camel, she left home in search of exciting adventures.

"Don't worry," said Bartholomea's mother to her husband, "when she sees water falling from the sky without warning, and the unbearable humidity makes her armpits sticky, she will come back and beg us for forgiveness."

Seeing tiny water droplets falling through the air roused Bartholomea's curiosity even more. Not only did she learn to refer to this phenomenon by its proper name, *rain,* she also found out the cold winds farther north turned it into a feathery substance called *snow*. The word seemed familiar. Long time ago, a man from her tribe was beheaded for uttering something similar. Perhaps he was an explorer like her, but chose to return and share his knowledge with his ignorant relatives. His execution inadvertently revealed the hidden meaning of an ancient proverb: *In the eyes of cowards, wonders come as threats.*

One day, resting at an inn during one of her journeys, Bartholomea met a husky sailor, whose chest was covered with strange tattoos.

He told her that way up north the weather was so cold, seawater turned into stone, and there were whole mountains of it floating in the ocean. She didn't believe him. Sailors often bent the truth for personal gain, especially in the presence of women. Nevertheless, Bartholomea took him to her room, and they started doing all those unspeakable things that compulsive travelers do when they stay in a place they don't intend to return to. As she stared at his broad chest bouncing up and down to the rhythm of her moaning, she realized his tattoos depicted a map with a sea route to an archipelago, marked with the letter H. In this very moment, seconds before Bartholomea climaxed, the fate of the Hyperborean Empire was sealed.

"Greetings, redheaded inhabitants of H," shouted Bartholomea, as her ship dropped anchor on the Hyperborean shore, "I have traveled the world and the seven seas, looking for your miraculous mountains of petrified water! It took me ages to find my way here, and I'm glad my journey is finally over."

"Liar!" said an illiterate fisherman, "you look younger than my own granddaughter."

Bartholomea rolled her eyes.

"Don't be fooled by my perky breasts and my innocent

smile," she replied. "Time flows slower for people in constant motion. My body might be youthful and attractive, but my mind is old and wise."

Like most prominent historical figures, Bartholomea was instantly assigned a nickname: *The woman that came out of nowhere*. Since the end of the Age of Discovery, every Hyperborean child was taught there was nothing beyond the horizon. Now that her arrival proved everybody wrong, people tried to approach the controversy with a sense of humor, although everybody realized a meaningful explanation was urgently needed.

Arnold the Easily Convinced, Emperor of Heaven and Earth, welcomed Bartholomea to the palace with open arms and the concealed hope he was just having a bad dream.

"Your existence doesn't make sense," he said, "yet your breasts are too big to be figments of my imagination."

"Your Majesty," replied Bartholomea, "I would gladly annihilate myself, so I can conform to your world view, which I find fascinating and quite comforting, but we both know that in this Universe nothing ever disappears without a trace."

"It would be quite rude of me to demand something like this from a guest," said Arnold, "but I urge you to help me find a reasonable explanation why our instrument of observation couldn't detect the lands you are coming from."

When Bartholomea inspected the retired Scepter of Knowledge, she immediately recognized its limitations.

"I know where the problem is," she said. "When it comes to such instruments, size is of uttermost importance. An eventual enlargement would allow you to catch a glimpse

of the lands that lie on the opposite side of the ocean, and if the weather conditions are favorable, even spot the mountains that lie beyond their shores. However, I must warn you that the successful completion of such a project would require a lot of resources and pose a serious economic challenge."

Arnold decided the risk was worth taking and immediately began a comprehensive upgrade, setting up to double the reach of the Scepter of Knowledge in less than five decades.

"Apart from resolving the Bartholomea paradox, this project will once and for all establish our empire as the greatest power in the Universe," announced the emperor.

The ambitious undertaking drew the attention of the Goddess of Ice. Seeing yet another of her creations succumb to the trappings of grandeur brought her great disappointment. She knew it was just a matter of time before the Hyperboreans point their improved instrument to the skies and catch her off guard in a delicate pose, forever undermining her authority. And while she had plenty of eggs to wreak havoc on them, something seemingly insignificant might survive the next thermonuclear explosion. Inevitably, someone would dig it out of the rubble and sow the seeds of another revolt. The Goddess needed a permanent solution.

For three days and three nights she plotted her response. On the fourth morning, she took a sip of her favorite tea, gargled for a minute, and spat into the ocean. Her saliva roused the salty waters. Out of their murky depths rose a magnificent island, covered in lush forests, teaming with fantastic beasts and wondrous birds. In its center stood a magnificent palace. Its ivory walls and stained glass windows extended all the way up to the sky.

"Such marvels are unworthy of the crude Earth," said the Goddess, "yet I would rather bring the skies down than allow gravel to contaminate my sacred realms."

And thus, she put on her most beautiful dress made from the silk of heavenly arachnids—a fabric so delicate and pure, even the mildest breeze could pass through undisturbed. She took residence in the palace, along with her thousand and one servants. They brought foods and drinks that had never touched the lips of a human. Their taste was so exquisite, it could drive a mortal soul to madness. When she had her fill, the Goddess retreated to the sprawling terrace of the palace and took a nap on a hammock of golden cashmere.

Across the Arctic Ocean, King Henry the Navigator, son of Arnold the Easily Convinced, by the grace of the Goddess, forever August, Enlarger of Empires, Subjugator of Horizons, Conqueror of Worlds, and Disseminator of Wisdom, peeked through the upgraded Scepter of Knowledge in search of new dominions. As he adjusted its focus, his eyes stumbled upon the bulging breasts of the Goddess. Blinded by lust and hubris, Henry took his divine mistress for a damsel in distress.

"I just discovered a wondrous island, whose queen seems rather melancholic," he said to his minister of important announcements. "I claim her as my most precious subject and declare her realms my personal protectorate, over which I shall rule justly and perpetually."

"Inhabitants of the realm," shouted the minister through

his loudspeaker, "It is my delightful duty to inform you that our most distinguished emperor just discovered a new land, ruled by a queen who doesn't seem to be in good spirits."

An hour later, Henry summoned his government.

"We live in times of constant change and they require radical decisions," he said to them. "After careful consideration, I have determined that our style of exploration is old-fashioned and needs urgent improvement. It is not sufficient to study the horizon from afar anymore. A modern ruler who takes conquest seriously cannot annex lands by mere observation. He must bravely set foot on them and plant flags in their soil. I have therefore issued immediate orders for the creation of a fleet, with which I shall depart on an expedition."

As soon as the ships were ready, Henry sailed for the island of the Goddess with a hundred of his best men. A fourth of them disappeared during a sea storm. Another fourth rebelled, demanding to go back, and were executed for mutiny. Three accidentally fell overboard while no one was looking. Twelve succumbed to food poisoning. Sixteen got drunk at a birthday party, fell asleep on the dock, and froze to death. Nineteen committed suicide because in the hassle of the initial preparations, nobody thought about bringing a counselor on board. Finally, after a long and perilous journey, in the Year of the Forlorn Geriatric Minks, Henry, the sole survivor of the first Hyperborean voyage of exploration, disembarked on the island.

"Welcome to the New World," said the Goddess.

Back home, the government, worried the emperor might have perished, authorized the minister of exploration to use the Scepter of Knowledge and search for the fleet. He followed the trail of dead bodies all the way to the island of the Goddess. There he saw his emperor, waving frantically, holding a big note in his hands. It said:

This place is awesome! You should all come over!

About the Author

Yanko Tsvetkov is a Bulgarian artist who lives in Spain, writes in English, and publishes books in Germany, France, Russia, Turkey, Italy, and China. He has visited several continents, passed through thick jungles, picnicked in scorching deserts, and booked a few taxis in busy metropolises. Today he leads a second life as a superhero that fights prejudice with his giant laser and his gorgeous cape.

Printed by Amazon Italia Logistica S.r.l.
Torrazza Piemonte (TO), Italy